THIS IS WHITE COUNTRY

BARBRA-LEE STEPHEN

For book orders, email orders@traffordpublishing.com.sg

Most Trafford Singapore titles are also available at major online book retailers.

Printed in Singapore.

ISBN: 978-1-4669-3450-4 (sc)
ISBN: 978-1-4669-3451-1 (hc)
ISBN: 978-1-4669-3452-8 (e)

Trafford rev. 01/25/2013

Tr**⚡**fford www.traffordpublishing.com.sg

Singapore
toll-free: 800 101 2656 (Singapore)
Fax: 800 101 2656 (Singapore)

To Altiyan Childs for his encouragement
and for his indomitable spirit. Much love.

And to my mother, Janet Stephen and
my sister, Callie 'Sparkles' Stephen
for their limitless patience and encouragement.

Son of Mine

My son, your troubled eyes search mine,
puzzled and hurt by colour line.
Your black skin soft as velvet shine;
what can I tell you, son of mine?

I could tell you of heartbreak, hatred blind,
I could tell you of crimes that shame mankind,
of brutal wrong and deeds malign,
of rape and murder, son of mine;

But I'll tell you instead of brave and fine.
When lines of black and white entwine,
and men in brotherhood combine—
This would I tell you, son of mine.

Kath Walker/Oodgeroo Noonuccal

CHAPTER 1

No white man walked past the cemetery on Angel Street after sunset, except Father Joe Macaffery, who liked to claim he wasn't really white: he was Irish! A cry had drawn Father Joe there late one night—a cry that would turn him from trusted priest into town pariah and would make the young black boy he found there the catalyst for the greatest scandal to ever rock Bindaree. The boy was curled on the ground, bleeding and helpless, his face a bloody mess. His right arm obviously broken. Anger boiled up inside the priest. Doing his best to ignore it, he concentrated on the boy. Anger had only ever gotten him into trouble and a chunk of his youth was held hostage to that emotion. Only time and guidance had taught him how to harness it, and his rage now simmered low inside him, like a pilot light.

He knelt next to the small body and reached out to stroke the boy's hair off his forehead. "Hey there, I'm going to get you out of here."

The child cringed away from his hand. "It's all right, lad. I'm Father Macaffery. I'm not going to hurt you."

He got no answer.

"Someone certainly did a job on you. I'm going to pick you up, lad. I'll get you to a doctor as quickly as I can. I promise."

The boy was small, and trembling as much from shock as from cold, the priest guessed. Father Joe took off his shirt and covered the child.

"What on earth are you doing here, lad?" he asked. "At this time of night you should be tucked up in bed."

Having left his car at the presbytery, and believing it to be quicker than calling for one of Bindaree's two ambulances, he carried the boy as gently as he could up Tully Street and into the Sisters of Mercy Hospital. The whole way, his soothing Irish lilt calmed the boy, telling him inane things, things his mother had once said to him when he was a boy and hurt. The half-naked priest with the young black boy drew plenty of glances before a nurse went to find a doctor.

"What's your name?" Father Joe asked him.

"Trey," the boy whispered into the priest's chest.

"Trey, is it? That's a fine name, lad. I'm going to need your number, Trey, so I can call your folks."

Trey gave his mother's name and number, and it was only then that he asked, "Where's Tommy?"

"Who is Tommy?"

"My brother. He left me. I don't know where he went."

"I don't know where Tommy is right now. You lie back and let Doc Wilson have a look at you. I'll call your mum. Perhaps she knows where Tommy is."

When the priest returned from making the phone call, the boy refused to be separated from him, until an hour later, when a harried looking woman barreled through the doors, spitting profanities. Alice King was just in time to hear Trey was being admitted and she was as happy about that as a drunk was with lemonade. Doc Wilson returned to confirm that Trey's right eye socket was broken and his retina detached.

"Your son needs to see an eye specialist," he told Alice, gesturing at Trey's eye now heavily padded. It meant a morning trip to Marsden via ambulance, one hundred and ten kilometers away. It was only when Doc Wilson told her that Trey's injury was so bad that he might lose the sight in his right eye that Alice finally succumbed to tears. She had done an admirable job of ignoring Father Joe until then too, but finally understood that the priest had rescued her son. Father Joe watched as her tough exterior collapsed under the weight of her stress, and she sat down next to him and wept openly.

"I don't wish to insult you, Father," she said sorrowfully. "Especially after what you did for my boy, but the kids that did this are white. I guarantee you. They saw a young black boy and their diseased brains told them to give him a whippin'."

"Trey didn't tell me who they were, I'm afraid, Alice."

"He doesn't have to tell me; I know. They're white. I tell you, I'm starting to hate this town, Father."

Father Joe said nothing. He wasn't insulted. Alice had to have somewhere to focus her anger, even if it was misguided. He sympathised with her concern for her child, even as he grew increasingly worried about the racial resentment gnawing at Bindaree.

A small, picturesque seaside town of six-and-a-half thousand people, Bindaree survived mainly on fishing and tourism. Trawlers dotted the blue morning and evening, coming and going in the twilight hours when the sky put on a riot of colours. The town was also a quick through-road to the mines up north, a place where miners and men seeking work came to flop for a night or two. Consequently, it had its share of pubs, and even some ageing sex workers, which, as some things must, at least remained discreet. The town's mayor, Grady Samuels, was a tubby, self-important little man whose main occupation was catering to his hypochondria. He turned a blind eye to inhabitants' vices, as long as the town profited in some small way.

However, five kilometres from town, at the end of Cutler Street, was a settlement he could not ignore. The folk who lived there called it, The Res, and it was in stark contrast to the sunny streets of downtown Bindaree. It was, simply put, a slum—home to the thirty or so families that made up Bindaree's indigenous population. Mayor Samuels may as well have been the slum lord for all the thought he put into cleaning it up. The Res's cheap, asbestos-clogged houses and vans had holes in the walls and few doors. The streets were unpaved, and the rutted, red-dust road known by the locals as "Coon Road" was littered with bottles and used syringes. Telltale signs of the slum's degradation. Alcoholism and drug addiction were rife. Kids grew up drinking, and sniffing solvents. Violence was the likely outcome of any disagreements. Most nights, at least one Res inhabitant was being patched up at the hospital. Worse, many of the children in The Res were abused, and nearly all of them were truant. While Res elders still gathered to impose social order, they were being increasingly ignored. Many of them were of mixed blood, a fact that caused them inner conflict. Hated by, and hating the whites, it was hard for them to acknowledge the pale blood of "whitey" trickling through their veins.

White residents of the town shunned The Res, unsuccessfully pretending it didn't exist. In recent months, that had become impossible. Gangs of Aboriginal children, some no older than ten, had begun to venture into the township proper to sell methamphetamine. Their shopfront was the cemetery, which sat on a bluff overlooking the ocean. From there, they terrorised the whites, who blamed them for every misfortune, fanning the flames of discord. It was a vicious, tragic cycle, and one that was becoming increasingly violent, as the attack on Trey King showed. The combination of illegal narcotics and white indifference had spawned an epidemic of racial hatred in Bindaree.

Alice King blamed white kids for the attack on her son, but she was reticent to discuss why her boys were hanging around the cemetery at night. While the truth was slowly extracted from fifteen-year-old Tommy, Father Joe filled in the blanks. Tommy, it seemed, had taken his younger brother to the cemetery, where Tommy helped deal meth. It was to be Trey's initiation. In the darkness, the cemetery was populated as much by the living as by the dead. A heavy mist, rolling in off the sea, provided a protective shroud for illegal transactions. Everybody in Bindaree knew the police had a "don't ask, don't tell" policy when it came to clandestine activities in the cemetery. Father Joe was a different animal altogether.

But on the subject of drugs, Tommy clammed up tighter than a whore in confession. The priest guessed the boy's bravado was hiding a deep shame at having taken flight, leaving his younger brother to be beaten.

★   ★   ★

When Father Joe came visit the boy the next morning, Alice and Tommy were sitting by Trey's bedside while he slept.

"How's the patient?"

"Hello, Father. They ain't caught them white boys who did it yet." Alice seemed even angrier this morning, and hell bent on repeating her accusations to anyone who would listen, as if the perpetrators could be found and punished by the sheer force of her will.

"I'm afraid colour doesn't mean that much to me, Alice, but beating up a boy Trey's age is a cowardly crime."

Tommy King's stare bristled with naked hostility. "He's asleep. He doesn't need your God stuff," said the boy.

"Thomas, be quiet. Sorry, Father. I did want to thank you for your help last night. Doc Wilson said you carried him all the way from the cemetery. You probably think I'm a terrible mum, but I didn't know the boys snuck out. We're going to Marsden with Trey in a couple of hours."

"I just wanted to know how he was Alice, and I don't think you're a terrible mother."

"Doc gave him something, so he sleeps most of the time. I'm afraid to leave him in case they get it in their minds to come after him again."

"I'd say the security in here is pretty tight, Alice." The father smiled, and then a frown crumpled his features. "Is Tommy missing school today?"

Alice sighed heavily, as if she were weary all the way to her bones. "Thomas and Trey don't go to The Potter School no more. I'm not sending them out for whitey to kick the shit out of them. Pardon, Father."

Tommy looked suitably smug at the delivery of this news.

"Won't they miss out on their schooling?"

"You don't seem to understand, Father. They could have killed my baby. He might lose the sight in his eye. I want to keep my boy's safe."

Father Joe looked at the too-small shape in the bed, his gaze lingering on the cotton patch taped over the boy's eye. He wasn't sure what made him ask, but he did. "If I can come up with a solution so the boys can be schooled safely, do you think you'd be interested?"

Tommy looked troubled. His dark eyes swung from the priest to his mother, who was caressing her sleeping child's hand.

"Don't reckon I want them schooling in town, Father. I'm sorry. You seem like a decent enough man, and I thank you for saving my baby, but I think the boys will be OK with the schooling they got. Most important thing my boys have to learn is to stay out of whitey's way."

Father Joe didn't argue; that would be useless. "I'm sorry to hear that. I'll pray that you can take him home soon."

"Thank you, Father. I don't want you to get the idea that we hate all people—just the ones that hurt my baby."

"I'm sorry this happened, Alice. Take care."

Father Joe left them at Trey's bedside with Alice continuing to damn white people in general and Tommy eating his brother's dry toast. Racial intolerance was among the many issues a priest had to deal with, he knew; he just didn't know how. One thing he did know: those boys belonged in school.

In Bindaree, Father Joe Macaffery was one of few citizens who could walk any street, at any time, confident he would not be set upon by either race. Black, white or strawberry, it didn't matter—you didn't fuck with him!

A gifted boxer in his youth, he was tall and muscular, and as confident discussing the subtleties of the bible (not that the good book contained many morally sensitive passages in his opinion) as he was punching a bag at the YWCA. He had started sporting programmes aimed at getting Bindaree's youth off the streets, and was also a member of the SES and volunteer fire department. He made an impression, did Father Joe; although whether it was a godly one was sometimes called into question.

There were a lot of questions when it came to him, and the man himself supplied precious few answers. He had driven into town three years ago, with another man's bible on the passenger seat next to him, and installed himself in the presbytery at St Bernadette's. Where he came from, nobody could quite remember. But that was all right because the father was a likeable character who quickly became part of Bindaree life. Besides, it seemed right there should be a sense of mystique surrounding the man who wore the collar.

The father left the presbytery that adjoined the white wooden church of St Bernadette's every morning at five on the dot, dressed in his wetsuit with his longboard under one arm. He walked down the esplanade at the bottom of Angel Street and out onto North Saxon Beach, where he claimed it was easier for him to hold parlay with the lord. He'd surf for an hour, and then return to the church to ready himself for mass or to set about visiting his needier parishioners.

That morning, he kept seeing Tommy King's defiant young face in his mind and his mind worried at the problem like a cat does at a piece of string. Finally, an idea crept into his head and, once there, refused to budge. When he went surfing the next morning, his mind was still flushed with it. He wanted to turn things around in Bindaree before he was forced to visit more kids in hospital. The rot of racism was exacting a toll on the town. He needed to do something, and there was only one person who could help him.

★   ★   ★

"Well, if it isn't the silver-tongued preacher. How you doin', Joe?" Ma Bess's voluminous frame filled the doorway of her rusty caravan. She was the most respected of the Aboriginal elders, a member of the Kuku Yalanji people to Bindaree's north.

Father Joe was glad he could count her as a friend, because he wouldn't have cared to have her as an adversary. He smiled. "Good, thank you, Ma. I've come to be blessed with some Ma Bess wisdom."

"If it's wisdom you're after, better back in your car and turn around, Father. But you're up for some smart-arse banter and a dirty joke or two, I can help out."

"You can do more than that, Ma. You're the lady. Your people here listen to you."

"Not so much anymore. The bashings, selling wiz to littlies, they're not my ideas, believe me." She reached into the folds of her caftan and produced a bottle of clear liquor. "Some white lightning, Joe?"

Father Joe shook his head. "Not when I'm on duty."

"I thought your types were always on duty?" She took a long pull from the bottle.

"Yes, that's so, but I often sneak in a Glenfiddich before bed."

"Makes up for the lack of sex, I bet." Ma laughed heartily, and Father Joe laughed with her, until he saw her face turn grave.

"Heard about you rescuing Alice's youngster. That was a very decent thing you did, Joe. Trey was lucky you were there. Apparently, you make quite an impression, stalking the streets of Bindaree at night with your shirt off."

"You've heard already?"

"Preacher, you gotta know by now that nothin' escapes this old woman. I've got eyes in the back of my head and a tongue that can make a working lady blush. Now how, pray, do we stop what happened to young Trey from happening again?"

"That's what I've come to talk to you about. I want the kids in The Res to be in school during the day. It might tire them out enough that they'll think twice about tearing up the cemetery at night, at least that's my hope."

Ma looked at him as if he were an errant toddler come to amuse her. She knew none of the Aboriginal kids enrolled at The Potter School actually attended. She also knew their schooling wasn't a priority for many of their parents. "Preacher, look around you." She spread a fat hand towards the town. "The pale faces hate us. You seriously telling me you're thinking of putting my kids here in school with whitey? I know you mean well, and God loves a fool, but you force my lot in with your lot and you're going to get a lot of bruises; or maybe you don't think bruises show up on black?"

"They wouldn't be with 'my lot' to start. I'd be teaching them myself. All their A's, B's and C'—in the church."

Ma clapped her hands and laughed at him. "Church? You're a ballsy sort; I'll give you that. Hardly any of the kids you'd be after have ever set foot in a church."

"It's not my intention to convert them to Christ."

"No? Bad at your job, are you?"

"No. I want them off the streets and concentrating on something other than booze and drugs. Then what happened to Alice's boy might not happen again. If they happen to trip over Christ while they're in there, it won't be me who pushes them. I promise."

Ma laughed at him again and the bottle disappeared back into the folds of her dress. "And you'd teach them your good self?"

"I'm a qualified teacher."

Ma raised an eyebrow. "Oh, I hear you're a great many things, Joe. You truly think you can teach them, though? The little buggers can be feral."

"What other white man are they going to listen to?"

"They mightn't listen to you either. I know you're chock full of noble intentions, but I can't see how this plan of yours'll stop the wiz, or stop a pack of whites using a black kid to wipe their shoes on."

"It might not, completely."

Ma grimaced and one eyebrow shot up higher.

"OK, it *won't* completely, but it's a start, Ma, and it is my hope it'll bring some of the kids around."

Father Joe realised this was where his plan floundered; it relied a lot on hope, and the inhabitants of The Res weren't great consumers of hope.

"You won't be the only one I talk to, Ma. I intend talking to the high school principal and the mayor."

"I'll tell you right now, that fool Grady Samuels is not gonna come down on our side of this."

"Our side, Ma?"

"Well, call me old and tired, but I could use some help with my people and long's past the point when I can do it all myself. Don't get too excited. I still have to talk to the parents and the other elders about this."

With that, Father Joe knew he had won. Everyone in The Res knew Ma Bess's word counted the most.

"I just knew as soon as I met you, Joe, that you were going to cause me aggravation. God, save my black arse from do-gooders!"

★   ★   ★

Mayor Grady Samuels was no fool, but he was a bigot. He leaned way back in his leather desk chair and stared at Father Joe Macaffery as if the preacher had just dropped his trousers in the mayoral office. Father Joe had not even been invited to sit.

"The church? You've got to be kidding me?"

"I've never been more serious. You've got an enormous problem in The Res, and I, along with some of the elders, want to try to do something to help fix it. We can reverse what's going on in this town, Mayor. You know about the meth and, you must have heard that Alice King's boy has been hospitalised. I want to do something before it gets worse, before it costs a life."

The mayor's thumbs, initially twiddling on his not inconsiderable stomach, were now clamped down on his desk. He stared at Father Joe through narrowed eyes. "First of all," he said, "the town is fine. It's them out there in that dump who come into town and fuck it up; and yes, I heard about the King boy. Regrettable, but that sort of thing goes on everywhere."

Ignorance always aggravated Father Joe. He told himself to stay calm, no matter how the mayor treated him. "It would never have happened at all if he hadn't been roaming the cemetery at ten years of age. If things don't improve soon, you'll have to put on another groundsman out there just to pick up all the syringes. Look, Mayor Samuels, I'm offering you something for nothing here. What can it hurt to try it?"

"It won't work. They won't come."

"With the support of the elders, I think they will," he said standing as straight as he could.

"They won't come," repeated the mayor, his thumbs once more rotating on his sizable belly.

Father Joe fought hard to keep the smile on his face. "So, I have your blessing to try it?"

Grady Samuels was openly sneering at him now. "You can have my blessing—and my undershorts, Father. They still won't come."

★   ★   ★

"How well can they read and write?" Principal Mike Potter of Bindaree Central School, colloquially known as The Potter School, asked.

When Father Joe had explained his plan to Mike, the principal came on board immediately, although he still had a lot of questions.

"Well, they can tag buildings with spray cans, beyond that I really don't know."

"Then you'll need primers to help assess them with literacy. In the meantime, I suggest an old favourite: *The Chant of Jimmy Blacksmith* by Thomas Keneally," and Mike scanned his sagging bookcases until he came up with his copy of the acclaimed novel. "You want to incorporate their heritage into their schooling. You should probably start by reading it to them in class. Then you know they've paid attention at least, and haven't just skipped over the whole book. Also, it will provoke discussion. We'll register them all at this school. As far as I'm concerned, the church is just another demountable classroom. I can supply some old desks and chairs. I'm afraid the board will have to be a chalk one though."

"Thank you so much, Mike. I hope to repay the kindness one day."

The principal smiled warmly at him. "Hey, if this works, that's all the thanks I need. I'm onside one hundred per cent,

Father, but I have to admit, I keep asking myself one question: will they come?"

*   *   *

Father Joe bought paper, pens and exercise books out of his own pocket, and obtained a copy of *The Chant of Jimmy Blacksmith* from the Bindaree library. Then he drove out to Bellington Road, not far from The Res, and commissioned a local Aboriginal artist, Missy Jenkins, to paint a sign for their fledgling school.

Its rules were stated simply:

1. No Drugs, Booze or Cigarettes at School
2. No Swearing
3. Be Respectful of the Teacher and Other Students
4. Nobody Leaves the Church Ground During School Hours (Hours: Mon-Thurs, 9 a.m. until 4 p.m. Half an Hour for Recess, Half an Hour for Lunch)
5. Remember There Are No Stupid Questions. Questions Show Your Mind Is Working!

Because the school was so understaffed, kids fourteen years and over would be judged as seniors and taught how to mentor the younger kids. To date, their influence had been initiating kids into selling meth, fighting, or smoking and sniffing aerosol cans until they passed out. Learning, Father Macaffery knew, would be an alien experience for them. He just hoped it would be an exciting one.

CHAPTER 2

There was one other friend Father Joe was counting on to help: Gunther Pearce. On weekday afternoons, Father Joe could regularly be found at the YWCA, sparring or coaching basketball for a group of troubled teenagers. Initially, the boys had cursed him, but now they all generally held him in awe. Father Joe loved spending time with the kids, watching them turn their lives around. One afternoon, he had witnessed one of the Aboriginal boys, Gunther Pearce—a tall, thin boy of fifteen— laughing at Neville "One Pot" Bellamy, the town drunk, who had been slumped outside the court. It was out of character for Gunther, whom Father Joe knew to be a respectful young man. The Father had slung an arm around Gunther's shoulders as they walked inside. When they emerged, five minutes later, Gunther just smiled sheepishly, avoiding the other boys, and sat on the bench.

"What did he say to you?" one of the boys had asked him later.

But Gunther had just shaken his head. In the months that followed, he never disclosed what had been said, and nor did

Father Joe. After that, Gunther had begun to spend more and more time with Father Joe, following him around like a dusky shadow. He was always eager to help and keen to pepper the Father with questions about God, religion, and his possible place in the world.

Father Joe genuinely liked most of the kids who took shelter under the umbrella of the church. Their minds were still pliant enough to run on faith, rather than on the obstinate reasoning that was often the downfall of adults. But it was hard to witness the passive neglect of their parents at times. Edith and James Pearce seemed content to let Gunther do whatever he pleased, as long as he obeyed the edict: "Don't Annoy The Father!" They were regular churchgoers and were always courteous and kind, but seemed indifferent to the needs of their only son, above the basic obligations of feeding and clothing him. It was little wonder the boy latched onto the first adult who took an interest in him. Gunther had a sunny, caring disposition. His gentle brown eyes would often fill when a kindness was paid him, and he came to love Father Joe with an acolyte's heart. It was rare that the Father didn't see Gunther at least once a day. He had become a fixture around Saint Bernadette's, and in Father Joe's heart, as well. Where you found one, you would most likely find the other.

One morning, while they were sweeping out the church, Gunther asked, "Father, I won't go to hell for making fun of old One Pot, will I?"

"First of all, son, don't call him that. Mr Bellamy is not a well man, and we don't make fun of someone with an illness."

Gunther stared down at his feet.

Father Joe stopped and looked at the boy. "Are you sorry for what you did?"

"Yes, Father. Very"

"And would you do it again?"

Gunther looked up at him in alarm. "No, Father."

"Those two questions I just asked you, if you ask them of every action you take, will show your principles. If you live by your principles, you'll be pretty right, I think. You made an error in judgement, son. But God welcomes those who are sorry for their mistakes."

"Even blackfellas?"

Father Joe smiled. "Well, the way I see it, Gunther, God could use a little colour up there."

★　★　★

The morning St Bernadette's school was to open, Father Joe was nervous. Clutching his board under his arm, he stumbled down to the surf, where Gunther was sitting on a flat rock listening to an MP3 player. The boy caught up with the priest when Father Joe exited the surf.

"Big day, Father!"

"I hope so, son. Are your folks OK with you schooling in the church?"

"They're cool. It's getting pretty dangerous for us at The Potter School. I think you'll make an excellent teacher, Father."

The priest's stomach somersaulted. "I hope so, Gunther. Nearly everyone I've talked to about this little venture has expressed the same concern: Will they come? Will they give me a chance?"

Gunther shot him a dazzling smile. "They'll come, Father!"

"How do you know?"

"Because, whether they know it or not, they need you!"

Gunther was right. The first three kids trickled in about eight-thirty, and the Father let out a sigh of relief. He watched Gunther's ebony face split into a wide grin as he ran to meet them.

At about eight-forty, Alice King dropped off Thomas and his friend Doyle Roberts. "You helped my son, so I'll give you a go."

"Thank you, Alice."

On the dot of nine, an old Hilux van drove up with Ma Bess herself behind the wheel. She spilled out nine children, turned around, and drove back to The Res without a second glance. For all his stated optimism, Father Joe had been truthful with Gunther—part of him had not been expecting anyone to show. He counted eleven students the first day; not as many as he had been hoping for, but maybe as many as he could handle.

A couple of the kids he recognised from his trips to The Res. Doyle Roberts, a thickset boy with unruly curls, and Tommy King were barefoot. Father Joe greeted them at the door and immediately suspected he was going to have a problem with Doyle. The boy emitted the pungent aroma of XXXX, and his bloodshot eyes did not quite meet the Father's. He had three fifteen-year-olds: Doyle, Gunther and Dean. The latter was a small boy with a perfectly shaven head and old-fashioned wire spectacles. He waved his hands expansively in the air when he talked, and for some reason, everybody called Mudguard. The rest, including Tommy King, Jessica Martin and Freddy Fingers, (whom Mudguard solemnly informed the Father was named for his habit of "borrowing" other people's goods and forgetting to return them) went straight into class with little enthusiasm. He could see how it was: Ma Bess and their folks had told them they were going to the church school, and their word was law.

With pursed lips, they studied the sign that gave the hours and standards of behaviour. Father Doyle had a couple of the older boys push the pews back to accommodate the desks, although Doyle and Tommy seemed content to sit on theirs. Father Joe decided he had to assert some measure of control, quickly.

"I'm Father Macaffery. Thanks for coming, guys." He looked at Jessica, the lone female. "And ladies. For four days a week, this will be your second home. As I'm guessing you don't sit on tables in your home, you're expected to sit on chairs while you're here." Tommy quickly got behind his desk, but Doyle sighed theatrically before he shuffled behind his desk, his eyes locked firmly on the priest.

Oh yes, you're the tough guy, thought Father Joe. *You're the one who's going to make my life interesting.*

"Now, the first thing we're going to do every morning is take rollcall. So I want you to raise your hand when I point to you, and give me your name."

Mudguard and Freddy Fingers were the only difficulties. They simply refused to be called anything other than their unusual monikers. In the end, Father Joe decided he had bigger battles to fight. Mudguard kept his hand in the air.

"What is it, Mudguard?"

"Are we going to learn God stuff all day?"

"A fair question. Before I was a priest, I studied for my teaching certificate. I'll be teaching you English, Mathematics, and some History. No God stuff, OK?"

The kids visibly relaxed, but the boy still had his hand in the air.

"Yes, Mudguard?"

"That's good, because my folk believe in the old ways."

"I appreciate that Mudguard. I promise to leave Jesus Christ out of the syllabus. One thing we are going to have, though, is a mentoring program. You older kids are going to help the younger ones."

There was a chorus of groans and expletives. Doyle put up his hand.

"Yes?"

"Why can't you just teach us the normal way, dude? Why do we have to help the little kids?"

"Thank you for putting your hand up before you asked your question, Doyle, but don't ever call me dude again. I told you my name. I expect you to use it. If it's too complicated for you, just call me Father, and you'll soon catch on to the way I teach."

He turned to the rest of the class. "I want each of you boys fourteen and over, and that includes the hungover Mr Roberts, to sit next to one of the younger ones. This is not a traditional high school, troops, everyone lends a hand."

Doyle looked sheepish. There began much chatter over the repositioning of desks within the church. Father Joe was intensely aware he was playing to a hostile crowd. These kids, with the exception of Gunther, wanted to be anywhere but in a classroom.

The day was a tough one. He seemed to be battling a mighty apathy. He took them to the Bindaree Library, signed them all up for library cards, and allowed them to borrow up to two books each. It was pretty obvious they were unfamiliar with the library. The librarian, Miss Walpole, frowned the entire time and kept emphasising the word "borrow." She seemed unimpressed when he told her he thought the kids had grasped the concept. That they came out holding something tangible seemed to buoy some of them. Afterwards, they did a simple spelling test so Father

Joe could gauge their abilities. Then he led them down to the water for a game of beach cricket. He was pandering to them, he knew, but he needed them to enjoy themselves, so that they would want to return the next day. Maybe they were off to a slow start, but Father Joe was intensely aware that the eyes of the community were fixed on his little white church, and that there were a lot of naysayers.

The next day was easier—once he disabused them of the notion they would be playing sport every day of the week. Some of them brought their library books with them, and he allowed them an hour to read while he tried to chart an engaging lesson plan. He noticed that Mudguard was reading a book on monster trucks, and smiled. *Whatever floats your boat*, he thought.

By the end of the week, he had only lost a couple of kids. When he enquired as to their whereabouts, the other kids rolled their eyes. "Doin' stuff."

Every morning, Alice King continued to drop Tommy and Doyle, who had started staring at Father Joe in a challenging way in class.

"Do you actually think any of this stuff is going to help us? I mean, shit, I know how to write well enough, and make change."

The kids all looked expectant. Father Joe had already singled Doyle out as the leader of the pack.

"Will learning help you? You bet it will. It's entirely possible you might want to get a job one day, buy a house, travel. What you learn here will give you opportunities in life, and please do not use that language in my classroom, Doyle."

"You must think all blacks are stupid," said the boy.

"Why would you say a thing like that?"

"I don't see any white kids here."

"As it happens, I don't believe in stupidity. I believe you learn if you are willing to learn. Is it true you didn't attend The Potter School because of the attitude of the white kids?"

"Yeah, they hate us!"

"Well, that's why you're here. You now have a school of your own; one where there will be no fights, no bullying and no slacking off, because if I'm spending my time teaching you, I damn well expect you to pay attention."

Another hand went up.

"What is it, Dean?"

"Mudguard, Father!"

Father Joe tried not to smile. "Forgive me, please. What is it, Mudguard?"

"What if we're not smart enough?"

He stood up before them. "Listen up, all of you. I believe that dumb equals lazy. I promise that if you try your best, your best will be good enough."

"I hope so, Father. My Dad says it's important I go to school. He doesn't care where. He's gonna whip my arse if I eff this up, if you know what I mean?"

"Your dad sounds like a smart man, Mudguard. I tell you what, I'm going to turn up every morning bright-eyed enough to teach. All I want is for you to turn up every morning ready to listen. Do you think you can manage that?"

Gunther's yes was the most immediate and enthusiastic, but it was eventually joined be a ripple of grim consent. Father Joe allowed himself to believe he had made a little headway.

★   ★   ★

The next day Doyle challenged him again.

"This sucks! You're getting us to do stuff you should be doing." Frustrated at having to check Freddy's spelling, Doyle erupted and threw the younger boy's book across the church. Nine faces looked up expectantly, curious to see what the weird white man would do.

Father Joe turned and looked out the window. Without looking at the boy, he asked, "Why do you say I should be doing it, Doyle?"

Doyle slumped in his chair and mumbled, "They don't pay us to mark the other kids work."

"I see. And that's your whole argument, is it?"

"It's the truth."

Father Joe continued gazing out the window. "Actually, Doyle, that's not the whole truth."

Doyle stared at him. The other kids looked at both of them.

"You see, Doyle, they don't pay me to mark Freddy's work either. I am not being paid to be your teacher. I am donating my time, because I feel you guys deserve to have someone in your corner. I believe you should all have a chance at a good future."

"You're not getting paid? Fair dinkum?"

"Nothing. You see, Doyle, I don't mind teaching you guys for free. I like helping people. I think you guys are a great bunch of kids. Of course, I'm not so sure about Mudguard." Father Joe closed his eyes briefly and nodded. "No. Mudguard too, I suppose."

Mudguard burst into giggles.

"While you might think I'm pretty strange to want to be your teacher for no pay, I'll tell you what I'm not, and that's a sucker. Under this roof, you will show me respect. Similarly, you will respect each other." He spun around and stared at Doyle.

"Now, get up, go over, and pick up Freddy's book. You can bring it up here for me to see after you've finished checking it."

Doyle collected the book. "Sorry, Freddy," he said.

The rest of the class breathed a sigh of relief.

★   ★   ★

On the fifth day of class, Father Joe had just begun to tell them about the book they would be reading, *The Chant* of *Jimmy Blacksmith,* when something crashed through the window. Tommy and Jessica, the closest to it, let out yelps of alarm. The rest of the kids leapt to their feet and surrounded an ordinary red house brick with a piece of notepaper attached to it via two rubber bands. Father Joe picked it up.

"Send The Black Monkeys Somewhere Else!" it read.

Everyone, including the Father, was shaken.

"Is everybody all right?" he asked. "Nobody cut?"

Jessica looked on the verge of tears. The rest were silent.

"Gunther, there is a dustpan and broom in the presbytery, under the sink. Would you get them please?"

The boy moved swiftly.

In a strangled voice, Mudguard asked what the note said.

"Troops, we just got a message from some good Christian displaying their displeasure with our new school." He showed them the note, watched their reactions. "What do you think we should do about this?"

"You're asking us?" asked Doyle.

"Yes, lad. I want to know what you think."

"Maybe we should just pack up and go home," said Tommy, no doubt remembering what a group of angry whites had done to his brother.

"I suppose we could, but then they've won, haven't they?" Father Joe watched them battling with themselves. No school, and life goes back to the same monotony that they were used to. Would sticking it out give them hope something would be different, that it would be something worthwhile.

"Couldn't we have school in The Res?" asked Doyle.

"Believe me, there are people in The Res who feel exactly like the idiot who threw this. No, I think we'll stay right where we are. We'll show people that it will take more than a brick to move us."

None of the kids looked especially tough at that moment. In fact, most looked as though they could run back to The Res right away.

Then, of all people, Doyle, spoke up. "It seems a crummy idea now, guys, and obviously it's got whitey's back up, but I agree with the Father. If we split now, and it is only a brick, for Christ's sake—sorry Father—it will only make us look scared. Do we really want whitey to think we're scared of him?"

"No way," said Freddy and the others agreed. Even coming from a boy who probably still registered over the legal limit on a breathalyser, Doyle had managed to do what Father Joe wasn't sure he could—not only getting them to stay, but as he prevailed upon them to act as one; as a class—he had turned them into one. Father Joe wanted to pick that brick up and kiss it.

The days that followed tested his patience. The kids were naturally doubtful and sometimes hostile, but they weren't slow. In fact, they threw so many questions at him that Father Joe wondered if he would be able to keep up with them. If they didn't know something, they let him know. Mudguard's raised hand became an in-joke that even he laughed at. Father Joe went to bed each night exhausted but happy. The mentoring program was proving a success. The kids learned quickly and through helping and teaching each other, they gained respect. When he saw Mudguard studiously marking Freddy's spelling, his tongue clamped between his teeth, Father Joe knew God had meant for him to do this.

Gunther was terrific with the other kids, and was quick to pounce on them if they looked like speaking without raising their hands first. Living in town, with parents who were active Christians, Gunther was always aware he was in a church. He frequently took kids like Doyle to task over foul language or folly. Surprisingly, it was Gunther and Doyle who kept the other kids in line. Doyle was a natural leader, and as Father Joe witnessed the effort Doyle made to understand new ideas, his affection for the boy grew. But Doyle could also be a handful.

$$\star \quad \star \quad \star$$

The school was three weeks old by the time they finished reading *The Chant of Jimmy Blacksmith*. Father Joe suffered through his class's initial groans and sighs patiently, his storytelling style gleaned from Sunday sermons. Eventually, they shut up and listened to the story. When it was finished, they all reacted differently. The book was undoubtedly violent. Jimmy Blacksmith was an ambitious nineteenth-century Aborigine who married a white women and wanted to be treated as an equal. When racial slurs were directed at his wife, he went on a rampage, murdering six adults and two children.

"He was dumb!" said Doyle. "Blacks have never gotten the same respect as whites."

"Yeah, that's a lesson you learn real quick," said Tommy.

After a long silence, Jess asked, "But it's getting a bit better, isn't it?"

All of the kids looked at her in horror.

"I mean, the Prime Minister apologised to us—to the stolen generation, I mean. He said that what they did to us was wrong."

"Christ, Jess," he could afford to," said Doyle. "It didn't hurt him any to do that. Most people think he's a bloody hero because of it. But fact is we aren't equal to white people in this country, because they believe they're superior. And that is never going to change. Jimmy Blacksmith had a sheep loose in his top paddock, if you ask me."

"What he did was cowardly, though," she said. "Killing women and children."

Doyle levelled an accusatory glare at Father Joe. "Yeah, what's up with that, Father? Why did you read us a book about a coward Aborigine who kills women and kids?"

"I read you that book because it's a true story, Doyle. It's a damn good book, and it has a lot to say about the expectations of both black and white people in society at the time. I'm not asking you to take sides. I'm asking you to see the bigger picture."

But Doyle's mind was already made up. "That's a racist book, Father. Who wrote it?"

"A man named Thomas Keneally, and I can assure you he isn't a racist."

"Is he black?" asked Tommy

"No. He's a white man."

"Well, there you go," said Doyle, as if that explained everything.

"I suppose, Doyle, if it offends you so much, you could always write your own book one day."

They all looked at him in mystified silence. The idea that could even be a possibility was as alien to them as green cheese. Even Doyle was at a loss for words.

Father Joe delighted in their reaction to the book and hoped to find another that would engage them as much. It seemed the more he gave them the opportunity to mull over an idea, the more they surprised him and themselves with their insight. It wasn't his considerable skill as an orator that made them listen, it was that they had finally been asked what they thought.

They slipped up occasionally. Doyle's language was colourful at best, and he had been twice caught with Mudguard smoking rollies behind the church at lunchtime. He apologised twice, and Father Joe forgave him twice. After all, wasn't he in the forgiveness business? The second time, he warned Doyle that another slip would mean expulsion from the school and being sent back to The Res. The humiliation would be enough to ensure he didn't do it again.

Lunch was supplied by Father Joe, the funds coming out of his own pocket. It usually consisted of canned soup or baked beans, and an apple or an orange. He didn't mind the expense, as long as the kids were happy and learning, and if he needed evidence of the school's success, he gained five more students the following month.

There were no more bricks; instead, the Sunday congregation was making its opinion known. Attendance had once filled the little church to capacity, but following the school's inception, it dropped off noticeably. One morning, while returning from The Res, Father Joe saw June Bradshaw—once an avid churchgoer who had brought him a butter cake each Sunday—attempt to walk around him.

"Hello, June. How are you? I haven't seen you for a while."

"No, Father Macaffery, and you won't, as long as you continue to desecrate God's church teaching those godless piccaninnies. Send them back to that dump. They only want to sell their drugs anyway."

Father Joe was surprised by the vehemence in her voice. "I can assure you, none of my students is selling drugs."

"And how do you know that? Asked them did you?" June stalked past him.

Father Joe was struck by the question. Indeed he hadn't asked them. He suddenly realised he needed to make a phone call.

★   ★   ★

He found his students huddled around Gunther's desk.

"I'm not saying," said Gunther in a plaintive tone.

"Oh, come on, Gunny. You're the only one who's been in there. I bet it's full of pornos."

"Even better," Freddy piped up, "he's got a hydro system set up in there, growing some mean ganja."

"He doesn't have any of that. If you truly want to know, he's got a cruiserweight boxing belt in a cabinet on the wall."

"Huh? I don't get it. Priests aren't supposed to hit people," said Doyle. "He said he was a teacher."

From the doorway, Father Joe cleared his throat and watched his kids scurry like frightened, guilty mice back to their desks.

"I'll admit I don't understand the interest, but if you want to know what's in my personal quarters, why not ask me? Before I was a priest, I was a boxer. When I decided I could live without the pain, I got my teaching certificate. I won the belt you're speaking of before I was a teacher or a priest. Any more questions? Because I'll answer them. You should know that by now."

Freddy held up his hand.

"Yes, Freddy?"

"Was it a knockout, Father?"

"Oh, it was a knockout all right. I fought Bruiser Carmody. Let me tell you, he was a big guy. If he had been any bigger, he would have been a heavyweight. But I beat Bruiser that night. Not because he was large or slow. I beat him because he had an extremely small bleed in his brain. It was so small that neither Bruiser nor his coach or doctor could detect it. I hit Bruiser Carmody twice, and then he was lying dead at my feet. He was the last man I ever hit. So, after that, to prove to everyone that I wasn't, first, a murderer, and second, an arsehole, I decided to spend the rest of my days helping people. I handed my life over to God, and I must say he's done a lot better job at running it than I ever did. I keep the belt to remind me what I'm capable of without God. So, no dope or pornos, Freddy, just a reminder that I once killed a man."

Fourteen faces stared back at him shamefaced. All of them seemed to be stumbling on the road their childlike curiosity had driven them up. Gunther looked agonised.

"I'm sorry, Father," squeaked Freddy. "But you make a hell of a good teacher. You're doing a terrific job teaching us, like letting us read that book about the gangs.

Father Joe had handed out copies of *The Outsiders* by S.E. Hinton the week before. He had shown them the movie first to whet their appetite. After that, they were jostling for a copy, all of which their benefactor, Principal Mike Potter, had generously supplied.

As Mudguard put it, "Father, it was really cool . . . It was . . ."

"I think the word you're looking for is great, arsehole."

"Doyle! Language!"

"Sorry, Gunny. Sorry, Father."

"Yeah, well it was great," continued Mudguard, as if he had not been interrupted. "I never much liked reading before, but I've kind of changed my mind about it. Anyway, Father, you're doin' a terrific job, honest."

"That's good, Mudguard, because this week you're having a paramedic come talk to you. You're all going to learn CPR, so that if you ever see someone—a mate, a brother, a stranger—keel over after using drugs, you'll be able to help. It might only take the Ambos ten minutes to drive to the cemetery, but what are you going to do in that time? Stand there and watch? Believe me, that will haunt you for the rest of your days. So, we're going to learn what drugs do to the body, and how to save someone who has taken something one time too many."

His students, as he had come to think of them, looked decidedly wary. It shouldn't have surprised Father Joe that Tommy spoke up first.

"If you're expecting us to dob on anyone, you're being majorly stupid, Father. You can go on and feel happy about helping us and all, but we'll be toast if we give anyone up to the coppers."

Tommy, in particular, had seemed less combative recently, and it hurt Father Joe to see the boy back on the defensive, freezing him out.

"I don't want names, Tommy. I especially don't want to know whether you've used drugs yourselves, although I hope you'd be smarter than that. If any of you are going to live in that world, I just want you to be prepared. Maybe I'm a little bit selfish. You see, I don't particularly want to lose any of you.

You're growing on me." He smiled sheepishly to signify the topic had been put to bed.

It took them a while to relax again. Over eight weeks of going to school at St Bernadette's they had come to be more respectful, and were rather fascinated by the Father. Priest or not, he was yet another white man trying to change their ways. The difference between him and others was that they were sure he was doing it to give them options, rather than to take them away.

★   ★   ★

Mayor Grady Samuels had heard the progress of the church school secondhand, from townsfolk who were less than pleased by its success. He had to admit he had underestimated the priest and the influence he had over the blacks. Samuels had thought none of the little golliwogs would turn up, let alone stay. Grady didn't much like being wrong, which made it a matter of pride. He refused to be made a fool of by a bunch of blacks and a priest who was a few screws loose. On that particular morning, the mayor had the beginnings of a migraine forming and a resting heart rate of 105bpm. Sure he was courting a significant stroke or heart attack, he was doing deep breathing exercises at his desk to forestall a medical emergency he considered a very real possibility, given he *was* doing the most difficult job in town. People didn't understand all that being mayor entailed. *Someone* had to govern while the blacks were learning their alphabet in the church and the whites were complaining and wanting them the hell gone. Meanwhile, Macaffery seemed to believe that, by virtue of his position, he could do whatever he damn well pleased. The priest was arrogant, and the only person Grady accepted arrogance in was the one person he refused to see it in—himself. Christ, even his own wife—an obese, simpering woman Grady held in the utmost disdain— thought Macaffery some kind of humanitarian hero for starting the school. Of course, a simpleton like Olive couldn't see the wider ramifications, even when he tried to point them out. She couldn't see Macaffery was disrupting the normally placid state of the town. As he held a cold pack to the back of his neck, Grady reasoned the priest's defiance had gone on long enough. It was time the mayor used his authority to shut the school down.

CHAPTER 3

Father Joe was sorting through the mail when the phone rang.

"Hi, Joe. Gus Passali here. Just checking up to see how my boy's going."

The older man's voice was enough to bring a smile to the preacher's face. He didn't call often enough.

Father Gus was a pug-faced, hard-boiled man, twenty years Joe's senior. He was also no stranger to lacing up the gloves. Although loud and brash, he listened and he didn't take crap from anyone save the Lord. In Father Joe's younger, darker years, when most people had written him off as an incorrigible, it was Gus Passali, with his unvarnished but infinitely fair view of the world, that Joe Macaffery had listened to. They had stayed in regular contact over the years and Joe knew Father Gus considered his student's rehabilitation one of his crowning achievements. It was Gus who had suggested Joe's move to Bindaree, thinking the slower pace of the seaside town might benefit the younger man's scarred soul. As usual, he had been right.

"Hello, Father. It's good to hear from you. The line's a bit noisy." Joe could detect a wheezing sound in the background.

"That's not the line, sonny. It's my oxygen! Too much whisky and too many cigars! The big guy can be ferocious when it comes to payback. The truth is, I'll be toes-up soon, and I just wanted to know that my star pupil is doing OK. How's beautiful Bindaree treating you?"

"Sorry to hear about your health, Father. I would come down there and be of some help to you, but I've got a mighty obligation here. It might even be a smart thing to get out of Bindaree for a while, but I don't want to let anyone down here. Give me a couple of days to think about it. Maybe I can come up with a solution. I could sure use some guidance about now."

There was a long pause at the other end of the line.

"Aha. And what are you running away from, sonny?"

"Hell, I've started something here, Father. Tried to do something good, and it has kind of backfired on me. It's turned into a bit of a rebellion. I know you told me to believe in myself and my faith, but I think by helping some people, I've managed to alienate an entire town." He told his mentor about the school, the sentiments of the white community, and of course, the brick.

"As much as I'd like to see you, Joe, you can't do a runner. What's the old expression? Fuck em' all and let God sort 'em out. Joe, I've known you since you were a young punk intent on doing maximum damage to yourself and the world, remember? All you wanted to do was knock me flat on my arse, something, if I recall, that even with your considerable talent, you were unable to do. You were one angry young man. At first, I thought it was just because you were a Mick. But I came to realise it didn't matter who was in the opposing corner. Inside the ring or out, you were fighting your father every time. You've come such a long way since then. You can't fuck it up now by quitting when the going gets tough. It sounds as if those kids need you."

Father Joe sighed and ran a hand through his hair. "We both know it doesn't matter what I do from here. No amount of atoning will make up for what I did. That anger is still there, below the surface. I can feel it."

There was another pause on the other end of the line, followed by the wheeze-suck of a ventilator, as if it were engaged in some obscene countdown.

"You committed a mortal sin, Joe. That damaged your soul, no doubt about it, but the rub is that it could have happened to any one of us. It could well have happened to me. I could always see a glimmer of the good man you'd become, and you've become that man, so stop being so hard on yourself. As the old adage goes: get off the cross, someone else needs the wood!"

"I still fear what I'm capable of, though."

"You know, that might always be the case. But it doesn't lessen the need of those young people. You can still do right by them."

"I know. I'm just saying. I pray every day for the Lord to take that old anger away, but so far my pleas have fallen on deaf ears."

"He's not deaf, sonny. He's given you free will. It's how he tests his faithful."

The older man's words felt like sunshine on Father Joe's face.

"You'll be OK, Joe. In you, I have faith. Hey, what do you think: if I'm still kicking in a fortnight, I'll give you a ring and check back up on you? Don't give up, sonny. I never taught you to throw the towel into the ring, and I don't expect you to start now, and don't worry about me, I'm an old fart who is used to taking care of himself."

"Thank you, Father Gus."

Meanwhile, his congregation continued to fall off. The wider community did not approve of the church school. Racial tensions were fierce, and his white churchgoers disliked the perceived notion that the priest preferred keeping company with Aborigines. Depressed and angered by the poor turnout in the pews, one Sunday morning in the middle of his sermon—a hastily scrawled treatise on showing compassion to your neighbours—he walked across the floor, picked up the infamous red house brick, and plopped it down on the pulpit. He did not refer to it in any way, but the congregation took it for what it was: a slap in the face, not only to whoever threw it, but to those who secretly applauded the act. The effect his action had was startling. A middle-aged woman broke from her knitting to watch him, then rose and stalked from the church, shaking her head. One of the commercial fishermen, a burly, red-faced man named Nigel Tomlinson, stood up from the third pew from the front and interrupted. "Father, I'd appreciate it if you wouldn't put that thing next to God's bible."

Father Joe stopped talking and looked at the man. He liked Nigel. He had, on a few occasions, shared a beer with him at the pub. Every word in his reply was weighed heavily before he let it pass his lips. "I appreciate your feelings, Nigel, but I think having this brick anywhere within the vicinity of the Lord's word robs it of any menace. It was a message intended for me, and I'm perfectly comfortable with it here until such time as its owner wants to step forward and reclaim it."

Unfortunately, this only honed Tomlinson's anger. "Perhaps its owner was trying to explain his exasperation at seeing his priest preferring to keep company with the bloody Abos than with members of his own congregation. Can you explain that to me please, Father?" Tomlinson remained standing. The church had gone deathly quiet as the two men faced off against each other.

Father Joe tried to smile. "Nigel, my feelings for the members of my congregation have not changed. I care about you all very much, but I don't feel as if I have to explain myself to anyone. I'm sorry."

"If you want to play it like that, Father, be it on your own head." The man grabbed his shocked wife's hand. "We won't be coming to church until you get your head right, and you had better do it quickly, because this town is losing patience—fast."

Father Joe watched as the fisherman and his wife stormed up the aisle. There was an awkward moment when the couple nearly collided with eighty-three year old Giselle Dresner's wheelchair, which was parked as it usually was in the aisle toward the rear of the church. The older woman looked saddened by the argument. The Father regretted the confrontation, of course, but he did not regret the action that provoked it. He would not be bullied by the citizens of Bindaree—a fact he had to make known to them. After the departure of the Tomlinsons, the paltry few left in the pews were busy studying their shoes in shocked silence or embarrassment.

"I apologise for the interruption. If you don't mind, we'll leave it here today. I would like to finish with the Lord's Prayer then we'll enjoy a coffee."

After the service, he mingled with what was left of his congregation (many had jumped into their cars the minute they said amen). One of his older parishioners, Mr Dufford,

approached, giving him the cleanest, whitest denture smile he
had ever seen.

"Great service, Father. It was a pity about the interruption
though, wasn't it? But, Nigel will get over it. You'll see." The
man shifted his feet in the dust. "Things are getting a bit sparse
around here, though. Aren't they?"

Father Joe said nothing.

Dufford went right on talking, misconstruing the preacher's
silence as tacit agreement. "Not me, though. Only this morning
I told Rose that it doesn't matter what might be going on in the
church during the week, it's a house of God on weekends."

"It's a house of God every day, Frank. All that's happening
on weekdays is that some young people are getting an education
they maybe wouldn't get otherwise."

"Yeah, but you've got to admit they're all darkies, aren't
they? They're not apt to learn much. They're low-minded
people, Father."

For the first time since his long-ago fight with Bruiser
Carmody, Father Joe wanted to hit someone. Frank Dufford was
grinning stupidly at him, looking, for all that was holy, as if he
expected Father Joe to agree with him. The priest's fists were
clenched so tight he would later find half-moon indentations
from his fingernails in his palms. He started at Dufford. "Go
home, Frank. Go home, right now."

With that, he walked back into his church and schoolroom.

To compound Father Joe's problems, Mike Potter came to
see him the next day.

"Does your class have room for one more?"

"I don't know if my parish has room for one more, Mike.
But we're not in the business of turning folk away."

"Good, because I have a little lady I'm truly worried about. Name's Lilly Price. She's fifteen. I don't think she'll know many of your kids. She and her parents live in town. She's extremely bright but has been a constant target for bullies. And she's extremely shy—I mean catatonia-type shyness, Father. She's so fearful of some of the kids she's been carrying a knife to school. But she's no trouble, just scared witless every day. If she stays where she is, the situation's got the makings of a tragedy.'

Father Joe spread his arms. "And you think she'll be better off here?"

Mike Potter had aged a good deal in the last two months. Father Joe realised he wasn't the only one paying a price for their little venture.

"Well, Father, at least she'll be with her own kind." He shrugged hopelessly.

"I'll take her, Mike. But do you really think we're doing the right thing? I'm not so certain anymore. Segregating them might be just another step toward prejudicing the whole town against them. I feel like we're setting them up to fail. We've got to find a way to banish the borders, not build them."

Mike smiled. "Well, if you would like to banish some of those borders, that's the other reason I'm here. I've got a soccer team in dire need of some healthy competition. Do you think your kids would be up for it? Understand I don't want this to disintegrate into a brawl between your kids and mine. A fair game for all, what do you say?"

"When would this match be, Mike?"

"How's a week from Thursday?"

"I'll let you know. I have to talk it over with them, but as far as I'm concerned, it's a yes. And Mike . . ." Father Joe broke off and put his hand on the principal's arm. "Thank you."

"You're most welcome, Father."

That afternoon, he asked his kids. "Who's up for a game of soccer next week?"

They looked up at him gratefully, seeking any reprieve from the mathematics problems they had been asked to solve. There was a resounding, affirmative chorus. The quiet came only when they were told whom they would be playing.

"Do you think mixing it up with the white kids is such a good idea, Father?" asked Doyle.

"As a matter of fact, I do, Doyle. Mike Potter has requested some help from us. Seems his kids need the practice. You don't think it could be fun?"

Doyle rolled his eyes and banged his head on the desk melodramatically. "Beggin' your pardon, Father, but I think it's about the craziest thing you've come up with yet. They hate us over there!"

"We're just going to have to change their minds about us then, aren't we? Show them we're not the black bogeymen they think we are. Principal Potter has assured me we're going to be treated fairly, and that there will be no foul play on their part. Think you could play an honest game without being too conscious that the poor devils are white?"

Freddy put his hand up. "I bags goalie."

"OK, Freddy. You're it. I also must tell you that you're going to have some spectators. Ma Bess and Alice King are driving us, and Gunther, your parents will no doubt be bringing their camera, so look sharp."

"I don't know about this, Father." Mudguard chewed on his lip. "What if they're out to bust us up instead of playing ball?"

"With Principal Potter and myself watching, I don't think that's likely. Now, I need to tell you a couple of things. You will not be argumentative, and you will not attempt to trip or hurt any of the white kids in any way. I want a decent, clean game. Remember, they see us as black, but as far as we're concerned on a sporting field, just as in this classroom, colour doesn't matter. We have our beautifully decorative brick right here to remind us if we lose our way. Another thing, after the game, win, lose or draw, I want you to go up to the kids on the other team, shake hands and say good game, just like they do on TV. That's called good sportsmanship. Do you think you can do that?"

There was rowdy consent.

"There is one final, but very important, thing I want you to do, when you're out there on that field."

"What's that, Father?" asked Gunther.

"Whip their butts."

⋆　⋆　⋆

Despite Father Joe beginning to think the divide between his kids and the community of Bindaree was impenetrable, the kids themselves were his greatest joy. He had to constantly remind himself their achievements were not his; he was only the Lord's tool. He just didn't know what it would take to make the town see them through his eyes.

Maybe it was time to visit The Res and Ma Bess.

Father Joe found her sitting in the same doorway and chatting with an older man in a tattered waistcoat. The man was hunkered down on one knee, gesturing demonstratively with both hands, but his hands flew down immediately when he saw Father Joe's old Ford pull up and he stared at the preacher with naked and inexplicable hostility. He said nothing.

Ma Bess was welcoming, although she didn't introduce her friend, which made Father Joe feel stupid.

"Preacher, bless your little old heart." Ma grinned up at him. "You've come to save us heathen savages. What is it now? Are you planning on switching every Stephen King novel and Playboy with that long-winded good book of yours?" She turned to her silent companion. "What do you say, Percy? Want your soul saved today? The Preacher here works cheap."

Father Joe couldn't help but laugh. He enjoyed these talks with Ma. But the man named Percy said nothing.

"You've got it wrong this time, my lady," Father Joe told her. "Today I'm seeking permission to educate some overly confident white kids."

Percy made a perfunctory hock in the back of his throat and spat into the dust, just inches from Father Joe's shoes. Bess took a sip from a bottle and offered it to Father Joe, who declined with good grace.

"So, Joe, you're too good to drink with us, but not to ask for my help."

"It wouldn't do for the kids to smell liquor on my breath, Ma."

"OK, spit it out. What's this about white kids?"

"My kids are playing a game of soccer against The Potter School next Thursday, and I was hoping you might drive us and that some of the parents would come and cheer us on."

Ma made a face and sighed heavily. "Are your brains pickled, Preacher? This has trouble spelled all over it."

"Actually, I don't think it does, but it sure would give the kids a boost if they had their folks there to watch."

"My God! For a preacher, you sure are a demanding son of a bitch. Leave it with me. I'll talk to some people." She smiled up at him, and the Father knew she would do her best.

The ageing man in the waste coat spat noisily again. Without speaking a word, he had managed to make his feelings on the matter crystal-clear.

★ ★ ★

One afternoon, as the kids were preparing to go home and Father Joe was reading through assignments, Gunther approached him. "Father, when are you going to go back to coaching the basketball team. I know you have a lot on, but the team still needs you." Basketball was to Gunther what surfing was to the Father. The boy was good, too. He had a terrific jump shot. Father Joe had been feeling guilty for letting it slide.

"I promise it'll be soon, son. Take pity on old men, we move slowly." He smiled up at the boy, but Gunther just nodded. He didn't get the humour for once. Father Joe realised he hadn't anticipated just how time-consuming the school would be.

"If I hear correctly, that's Ma's bus come to pick you all up, so scoot."

Ma always dropped Gunther off at his house before returning to The Res in the afternoons. They didn't say it aloud, but some of the kids were worried about walking around town on their own. While the other kids whirled around the church, gathering up bags and skateboards, and preparing to flee for the weekend, Gunther remained.

"Father, I know what I want to be when I'm older."

"That's great, Gunther! You're halfway there. What is it?"

"I want to be a father!"

"Don't you think you might like to get married first?"

"Not that kind of *father.* I want to be a Father like you."

Father Joe suddenly discovered a lump in his throat. Looking at Gunther's innocent face, it was hard for him to maintain his composure. *Not like me, son,* he thought, believing he was damned for his past mistakes.

"You're a good boy, Gunther." He picked up a New Testament off the shelf behind him. Taking a sharpie, he wrote Gunther Pearce on the inside flap and handed the book to the boy. "You'll need one of these then."

Gunther's face broke into a huge grin. "Thank you, Father."

"Now you better get on home."

"I'll see you at the beach in the morning, Father."

"You don't get tired of watching an old man tumble around in the waves?"

"No. It's the best part of my day."

That lump was getting harder to swallow.

That night Father Joe was trying to mark schoolwork and seek inspiration for the coming Sunday sermon simultaneously; it wasn't working. Lately, his nights had been as busy as his days. He was contemplating a whisky when the phone rang.

"I apologise for calling so late, Father." Mike Potter sounded worried. "But I knew you'd want this information."

"What's up, Mike?"

"I know you're interested in the drug problem here in Bindaree, especially as it seems the dealer is using kids from The Res to help him sell his crap."

Father Joe suddenly wasn't tired anymore. "Mike, if you know something, just tell me."

"I've seen an Aboriginal man at the gates of the school twice this week. Both times it was as the kids were going home.

He was talking with some of the younger kids this afternoon, handing out cigarettes. I found a Year 7 kid with a butt in his mouth! I don't know if he gave them anything else. I was going to confront him today, but he took off on a motorbike the instant he saw me. Shot me the finger. The guy looked like trouble, big time. I'm going to hold an assembly tomorrow to warn the kids. You might want to do the same, Father. I don't know how to explain it, but the whole scene smelled bad."

"Of course. And you've never seen him before?"

"No, Father. I got the feeling that if you saw him, you'd remember him."

"Thanks for the warning."

"You're welcome. The way I see it, you're doing a marvellous job with your kids, I don't want anyone screwing it up for you."

"I'll ask around The Res tomorrow." Father Joe didn't like the sound of any of this. "See if anybody knows this customer."

"Good. I'll talk to you soon, Father. 'Night."

★   ★   ★

"Victor Dumagee!"

"You know him? Well, what are you doing to catch him, or at the very least chase him out of Bindaree?" asked Father Joe. He was seated around a campfire in The Res next to two of the elders: Jeremy Pindari, who did most of the talking, and John Kutukutu, who seemed sullen and suspicious. Ma was the only female. She had told him he could attend this meeting as long as he, in her words, "didn't babble on about Jesus." It was an opportunity he couldn't pass up.

Ma Bess offered the fire more burning eucalyptus leaves and gazed at the dark faces of John and Jeremy, men whose age was displayed in the lines of their gleaming, leather-worn faces. Both were drinking beer, a slab resting between John's feet. They had offered a stubbie to Father Joe, but he had declined.

"I don't know him personally," said Jeremy. "I can live without the experience. He's trouble. I hear from some he's Wiradjuri."

He looked to Father Joe and explained, "Wiradjuri are river people. Proud people. Trodden this land for thousands of years. When whitefellas came and took away their land, wrecked what remained, Wiradjuri became warriors of our people. White man with his gunpowder won in the end." Jeremy shrugged, as if to indicate this was not surprising.

"Wiradjuri, my arse!" said Ma Bess. "This Victor is an ungrateful whelp. He's a tick, sucking the blood out of people, black and white. Using kiddies to sell drugs to other kiddies! I for one am sick of it. Far as I'm concerned, he comes from nowhere, and he should go back there!"

"But, if you know who he is, why don't you stop him?" asked Father Joe.

"Because he's dangerous, Father. He moves around a lot, and he's helped by those who have a taste for the wiz. Exploits them—same as he exploits the kids. You know a lot of the people who live here, Father. They want their drugs. They don't want change: it frightens them. They're not about to give him up."

"What about the police?"

Jeremy stared at Father Joe from under a fringe of wiry, grey hair. It was a look he might have given a person of diminished mental capacity. "Fact he's been operating this long, means he's probably bought off the coppers. You don't see them in here busting down any doors, do you?"

They were all silent for a while, only the fire crackling in front of them.

Ma Bess studied Father Joe carefully. "Don't you even think about it, Preacher! You'll end up banged up or dead, or both, and I don't want that on my conscience, you hear me?"

"I didn't say anything, Ma."

"I know, but you're thinking it. Tell me I'm wrong."

He gave her a lopsided grin. Even when he tried to conceal his thoughts, Ma would ferret out the truth, as always. "You're never wrong, Ma."

Ma waggled her finger at him. "You stay out of this, Joe."

"Ma, I can get rid of this Victor. Have a little faith in me, won't you."

Father Joe was sure Jeremy's look was of sorely tried patience.

"I applaud your passion, Father," Jeremy broke in. "And I understand your goal is to help our kids so they get some learning behind them, and maybe a good job that'll let them run as far as they can from The Res and make good lives for themselves."

He had Father Joe's attention now.

"And I don't want to bust your balloon, but if we haven't got Dumagee under control by now, what makes you so sure you can do it?'

"Let's just say I can be very persuasive when I have to be."

Ma laughed. "Well, that much is true. You always manage to enlist me in your latest crackpot scheme. But listen to me for once, please Joe. This ain't a wise move. Victor Dumagee is a wild man. You do this, you should know he has no regard for anyone—black, white or indifferent. This is not the kind of man you can reason with."

"Let me try. That's all I ask."

Jeremy looked doubtful. "You do this, and it'll be the first time I'd be rooting for a whitefella. How strange is that? But, Father, don't you think this might be a little too much, even for you. You're already teaching the kids, and we're grateful—the majority of us, anyway. We know you're taking shit from whitey for helping us. If you're committed to doing this, there's something you should keep in mind."

"I'm listening. What is it?"

Jeremy stared straight into the fire as he spoke. It embarrassed him to say these things to a priest. "Father, whitey won't change his opinion of us, no matter what you do. I worry what might happen to you, spending so much time with us."

At last, John spoke up, and they were all surprised at the contempt in his voice. "Just what makes you think you've got the balls to dispatch Dumagee? You make a trip out here twice a week and you think you *know* us? You don't know nothing about our troubles. I've seen your type before. Another do-gooder who'll be burnt out in six weeks. Then that'll be the last we'll see of you. Oh yeah, you whites have been so very good to us. Killed eighty per cent of us in the first century of invasion and now you're slowly doing the same to the rest? So I'm sorry if I don't roll out the red carpet for you, Father. Far's I'm concerned you're just another whitefella trying to salve his guilty conscience."

"John, you forget yourself." Jeremy's voice rumbled deep with reprimand. "We don't talk to guests like that, white or not!"

Father Joe's blood was heated after listening to the man berate him, but he spoke calmly. "No, Jeremy. It's all right. Let the man speak his mind if he feels he must, but know this, all of you"—he levelled his gaze straight at John Kutukutu—"I won't be judged for actions others have taken long before I was born. Despite my unfortunate colour, I don't feel guilty. I promise I won't be quitting in six weeks. I'm not a quitter by nature."

"If you're expecting an apology, you'll have a long wait, Father. I won't apologise for speaking the truth."

"Then say nothing at all," said Jeremy. "This man is trying to help our children, and he's doing it at personal cost to himself." He turned back to Father Joe, who sat in embarrassed silence. "Father, I'm sorry. It's just that help from white people has always been conditional for us. Most times, we end up worse off than when we started. But Ma vouches for you, and that tells me a lot." He stared into the fire, which had burned down to embers. "Maybe you should be content to help us by educating our kids. They tell me you're an excellent teacher. Victor is really our problem to sort out."

"Jeremy, with all respect, it's not that simple. It doesn't matter how much I teach your kids. If there's some predator, like this Victor, out there hell bent on trashing their lives, all I've taught them will be in vain. So, I'm sorry," Father Joe said and turned to look at Ma Bess, "but I've got a date with this guy."

Ma Bess looked from John to Jeremy helplessly. "See? Now do you understand what I have to put up with? This white man's plum crazy!"

"He might be crazy, Ma. But he might also be the best chance to get rid of Dumagee, slim as that chance is," Jeremy said.

"Well, I say you're all crazy then." Ma snorted. "Any more beer? I'm going to get drunk and pretend this conversation never happened."

★   ★   ★

On his third reconnaissance mission to the cemetery, Father Joe finally encountered Victor—a tall, skinny man with a shaven head. Victor had received his "education" at the Tenderwood Home for Boys and the Marsden Correctional Centre. He was as black as pitch, with pupils the size of dinner plates. In daylight, you could see the trackmarks and sores that punctuated his arms. It was a sad truth that nobody liked Victor, and Victor didn't much like anybody. What he did like were drugs, and the money they brought him.

Father Joe walked through the cemetery plots with confidence, making a point not to be too quiet about it. He didn't want to surprise anybody, particularly not someone who was unstable and hooked on drugs. He found Victor kneeling at the entrance to an old crypt. The dealer was shuffling through a dozen or so dime bags and talking into a mobile phone. When he saw the Father, he stood, stowing the bags in a cigarette packet.

"Whoa there, Father. What do you want here at this time of night? I thought you dropped your load out here during the day?"

Two boys with him, who couldn't have yet been fifteen, giggled at his joke.

"Victor Dumagee?"

"That's me, dude. What can I do for you?"

"My name is Father Macaffery, not 'dude', and I thought we might have a word, Victor."

"But if I talked to you, would I just be talking to you, or would you have the loudspeaker to the man upstairs switched on? 'Cause I'll tell you true, Father, I just want to go about my business without any interference, you understand?"

"Oh, I understand. The trouble is: your business is fucking up this town!"

Victor stumbled back, a parody of surprise. "Christ fellas! Did you hear the mouth on the Father? He fucking swore at me. The last time someone swore at me like that, Father, I stuck a pen knife in his eyeball." His hands jittered wildly as he spoke.

It was clear Victor was as jazzed as his clients, and Father Joe realised there was no reasoning with him. Victor Dumagee was morally bankrupt. If the world were just, he should have been bouncing off the walls of a rubber room. Nonetheless, the Father was determined to deliver his message.

"I want you out of this town, Victor. I know you're using kids, like these, to hock your stuff. I want you—and your shit— out of this town."

The two kids, taking in this exchange intently, never moved from Victor's side.

"That just may be, Father. But I don't think that's going to happen. This is my home too, you see, and I don't much like you coming into my house"—he spread his arms, as if to encompass the whole cemetery—"and telling me what to do. In fact, I'm sort of the landlord around here, and I say it won't fuckin' do."

"You're screwing up these kids' lives, Victor."

"Hey man, they have a choice. Everyone has a choice. Even you, Father. Now, why don't you *choose* to fuck off out of here, or I'll make you a holy ghost yourself!" Victor pulled up his T-shirt just enough for Father Joe to see the butt of a handgun sticking out.

"I don't think you understand me, Victor. Gun or no gun, I want you gone from this town, and if I have to come back, I will make that happen. I hope, for your sake, you decide to get on your bike and leave."

Before Victor could say anything further, Father Joe turned on his heel and walked out of the cemetery. With each step he took, a foreboding crept over him. It made him believe the little scene he had just played out with Victor was small indeed, compared to what was coming.

★   ★   ★

On the afternoon of the soccer match, the trouble did not come from the quarter he had expected it to. When Ma Bess pulled up in front of St Bernadette's to collect the kids, Father Joe noticed Doyle wasn't wearing any shoes.

"Doyle, where are your trainers?"

"He doesn't have any, Father," said Gunther.

"Shut up, Gunny. It's none of your business. I've been kicking balls barefoot my whole life, Father. It's no biggie."

Father Joe sighed and entered the presbytery. A minute later, he emerged with forty dollars from Sunday's collection. He sincerely hoped it had come from the pocket of Mayor Grady Samuels. "C'mon Doyle, we're going to buy you some goal-kickers. We'll see you there in about an hour, Ma." He gave her a thumbs up and grinned when he received one back.

"C'mon kids," she said. "Let's haul arse."

The priest and the boy drove to the local K-Mart, where Doyle picked out a pair of white runners with a flashy blue racing stripe. "Are these OK, Father?"

"If they fit, Doyle, then they're OK."

When he pulled up at The Potter School, Mike's students were still inside. Ma Bess had corralled his kids onto the bleachers, where they were shifting around nervously as if they had fire ants in their britches. Mr and Mrs Pearce were there, and he saw a smiling Gunther wave to them. Alice and Trey were sitting with Mudguard's father. Chip and Sue Roberts were also there, and Chip was drunk. Not *When Irish Eyes are Smiling* kind of drunk, either, but mean and spoiling for a fight drunk! And then Chip spotted Doyle, proudly wearing his new shoes. "Hey, where'd you get the shoes, boy?"

Doyle and Father Joe joined the others. Doyle's face twisted into a grimace of misery.

"I said, where'd you get the shit-kickers, Doyle? Answer me, boy!"

"I don't think the Father wants that kind of language around the children, Chip," said Ma.

"The Father? Oh, woe is me, it's the bloody Father's opinion I need now, is it Ma?" He walked over and slapped Doyle in the back of the head. "Where'd you get the fucking shoes, Doyle? I didn't get them for you, that's for sure."

"The Father got them for me," said Doyle, staring at the offending shoes.

"The Father! The Father! That's all you can bloody talk about." He turned to Father Joe. "Hey, prissy boy, come and get your shoes." Knocking Doyle to the ground, Chip wrenched the shoes off his feet and flung them at Father Joe just as Mike was leading his kids on to the oval.

Mike sized up the situation quickly. "All right, my kids, you need to loosen up. Give me two laps around the oval." He turned to Father Joe. "Any of your kids need to warm up, Father?"

"You bet, Mike. Thank you. Troops, you follow the Potter kids, while I sort out this mess." He picked up the sneakers and walked calmly over to Chip. "I'm truly sorry if I overstepped the boundaries, Mr Roberts. You can take these back if you want, or you can make a donation to the church. Meanwhile, I hope you have no problems with Doyle missing the match. All the kids need the proper footwear. You're welcome to sit and enjoy the game, as long as you don't hit the boy again."

Chip lurched forward, within swinging distance of the priest. *He won't hit me, though,* thought Father Joe. *Men like Chip Roberts only pick on women and children.*

"Piss on your game, pretty boy. And piss on your fuckin' church too. If Doyle ain't playin', we're out of here."

"Oh, Dad. C'mon, please."

"No 'Oh, Dad.' Get in the fuckin' car, Doyle."

Following another swipe, which thankfully did not connect with his head, Doyle did just that.

As the Roberts family drove off in the direction of The Res, Ma Bess strolled up to Father Joe. "Well, that was a lot of fun, Joe. What do you say we have us a game of soccer now?"

Mike called the two groups of kids over. They were eyeing each other, and the scene at the bleachers, nervously.

"OK, St Bernadette kids, run left to right. Jess, do you want to step in for Doyle?" asked Father Joe.

"Will do, Father," said the girl.

"Mike, it's your place, do you want to ref? Just call it as you see it. My students, remember what we discussed and do me proud, OK?"

Mudguard saluted him comically.

"Will do, Father."

After that, the game was something of an anticlimax. It went off without a hitch. A ginger-haired kid from The Potter School was first to score. Then it was Gunther's turn, and Jessica finished it off with a goal three minutes before full time. His kids were ecstatic. Afterwards, they stepped forward to shake hands with the other team. Father Joe could see how shocked Mike and the white kids were by their conduct. Everyone helped themselves to oranges and cordial while Gunther showed one of the white kids how to head the ball. The game had been a success. Everyone agreed they should have a rematch the following week. Father Joe had never been prouder of his students. His joy was tempered only by his concern for Doyle.

★   ★   ★

"I hate him!"

"It's wrong to hate, Doyle. All it does is poison you."

They were sitting on the church steps, in the sun. Doyle had come to school wearing his new sneakers, and with an eye so swollen he could barely see out of it. He also reeked of alcohol. Father Joe's heart went out to the boy.

"Beg your pardon, Father, but you don't know what it's like."

"You think I don't know, Doyle? You think I don't know what it feels like? When your father comes home at three in the morning, roaring like a wounded bull. Trampling all your mother's daffodils because he's too damn drunk to find the path? How it feels to be up comforting your mother and then to have to creep back to your room. The shouting. Things being broken. How you have to be especially quiet the next morning because daddy has one of his headaches."

Doyle threw the bit of bark he had been playing with into the garden, giving Father Joe his full attention.

"What it feels like when you see the bruises on your mother, but you're not able to do anything about it, because you're only twelve—no threat to a man of forty with a bellyful of barley. Oh, I know, Doyle! I know real well. It feels cruel. It feels like you've been shafted, but those are the times to pray, not to hate. Remember, Doyle, God is a powerful ally. And when you're older, try your best not to walk in your old man's shoes. That definitely starts with not coming to school smelling like a brewery. When you do that, lad, you're disrespecting the other kids, me, and most of all, yourself."

The boy shrugged, his head down again. He seemed to be studying the pavement between his feet.

"I'm sorry, Father. My father says there are flowers and weeds in this life and that I'm one of the weeds. Says he never should have done it without a raincoat."

Father Joe smiled at the boy. "I don't believe that for a minute, and neither should you. I wouldn't spend so much time talking to a weed, would I?"

"I don't know, Father. Excuse me for saying this, but sometimes you can be a real, odd dude."

"Oh, you're right about that, lad. A wise man once said that it takes a while to learn to live in your own skin, so I guess I've still got some learning to do too."

"Did Jesus say that, Father?" asked the boy.

"No. Jon Bon Jovi."

CHAPTER 4

Father Joe had two visits that afternoon. One was welcome; one was not. Mike Potter drove over with Lilly Price, the young lady he had told Father Joe about. The girl was uncommonly pretty, but alarmingly shy. A fine-featured waif of a girl who Father Joe could see would grow to be a real beauty.

Father Joe's instincts told him to put her at the back of the room, where she wouldn't feel everybody else staring at her. There was some rearranging of desks until the girl was finally seated next to Gunther, whom she was friendly with from their time together at The Potter School. Doyle's machismo rocketed into the stratosphere in the presence of a pretty girl. He was barely controllable. Until now, Jessica had been the only female student, but in her feisty way she was able to dish it out and to take it. Father Joe told himself that Lilly needed his help if she was going to survive the unorthodox methods he employed at St Bernadette's School.

His second visitor would prove a thorn in his side. Mayor Grady Samuels rapped loudly on the church door and strode in, giving the class a robotic, politician's "Hello." Then he turned to Father Joe. "I was wondering if I might have a quick word, outside?"

"Certainly. Mudguard, you're in charge." The great whoop from the boy and the laughter that followed them outside made the Father doubt anything like work would be accomplished in his absence.

"Do you do that often?"

"Only when I'm not in the classroom."

The mayor nodded, as if he had predicted chaos and not been disappointed.

"I've been hearing some worrying things, Father. Apparently, you organised a soccer match where a boy was assaulted. I was told there was a drunken black there, invited by you, and that you're thinking of doing it again."

Father Joe's heart sank. "Was that a question, or a summary?"

"Don't be a wise-guy, Father! Everyone expected this little experiment with the darkies to have blown over, but now people have legitimate concerns for their children's welfare. Now, you did your best. You got some blacks a library card. Good for you! Now, shut this nonsense down. Or I will."

Father Joe could see a vein throbbing in the mayor's forehead. *I wouldn't want a wicked man's blood pressure*, he thought. "Listen, Mayor Samuels, I don't know if you've talked with Mike Potter, but the children are all enrolled in his school. This is just a division of it. I promise there was no real threat to the children at the game. Just one bad drunk, who went home when he realised he wasn't wanted."

"There will be zoning laws. Things like that. I could get on the phone right now to the Board of Education and have this church cleared out." The mayor's face turned ruddy.

For the first time, Father Joe realised just how little provocation it would take to push this man over the edge. "What concerns me most is why you would want to? We're not hurting anyone here, Mayor Samuels. As for the board, I think they want every child to get a decent education, regardless of colour."

The mayor looked at him mutely. "Why are you doing this, Father?" he eventually said.

"Because it needs doing."

"Do you really see any future lawyers or architects in *that* lot?" The mayor asked snidely, pointing to the church.

He has a vested interest in seeing the school fail, Father Joe realised. *He calls them blacks. He calls them darkies. It doesn't register that they are children.*

Not getting anywhere with his threats, the mayor suddenly changed his gambit, catching the priest unawares. His tone was softer, less confrontational, and thick with conspiracy. "Father, its Thursday. Pension day! What would you normally be doing on a Thursday morning, if you weren't here?"

Father Joe suddenly remembered Giselle Dresner. On Thursday mornings, he picked up her groceries for her. She phoned her order through to Max's supermarket and Father Joe would pick it up and deliver it to her house on Canal Street. Quite often, he would stay for a cup of tea and a game of chess. He had totally forgotten about Giselle these last two weeks, and she hadn't phoned to remind him. He could think of no other reason for her silence than that she, too, disapproved of the school. He had always thought of her as highly refined and intelligent. He hated to think it might be a veneer masking a dumb prejudice.

"It seems I owe Ms Dresner an apology. I'll visit her this afternoon, after school is out." He hated that Grady Samuels had snuck a punch in below the belt, but there seemed nothing he could do but cop it sweet. The mayor looked particularly pleased by Father Joe's discomfort.

"My point is, Father, you can't be everywhere. You can't be all things to all people. As an elected official, I know, believe me. I want you to think about what you are doing here. You saw Mr Tomlinson's anger the other day. If you continue, I can promise he won't be the only voice of dissent. In the meantime, it might be best if you don't take the darkies to The Potter School again. Mike Potter is a lovely man, but he's not a strong man, not like you and I. Do you understand, Father?" The mayor, happier now that he thought he had won the fight, if not the battle, patted him condescendingly on the shoulder and bid him good day, for now. The mayor walked back through the church, giving the children a jovial goodbye that sounded as phony to the priest as the fat little rooster's concerns.

"What a colossal arsehole," Father Joe said, just as Gunther walked out the door.

"Father!"

"Sorry Gunther, I didn't see you there. But sometimes you just have to call a spade a damn spade."

"Can I call him that?"

"You most certainly cannot. Not until you're older and you can understand just what makes one. Now what is happening in there?"

Gunther gave him his widest, sunniest smile. "I think you better get in there, Father. Doyle and Mudguard are going to go at it."

Father Joe sighed, but he also smiled. "I guess I better. C'mon, son."

CHAPTER 5

Giselle Dresner was a small, neat woman with a soft face and a graceful manner. Her lapis-blue eyes radiated with contained energy and intelligence. Father Joe had spent many afternoons here in her living room, discussing the books that lined the walls and often losing to her at chess, which Giselle played with the intensity of a grand master. Infirmity may have caught up with her physically, but her mind was as sharp as Ma Bess's tongue. His neglect of this particular parishioner and friend weighed heavily on him. Giselle's partner, Eve, had died of pneumonia two years before, and Father Joe knew she relished any time spent in the company of friends. She had answered the door as her usual polite self, and her smile seemed genuine. Bug, her small ginger cat, had scooted between Father Joe's feet, to leap up onto his mistress's lap.

"Bug, let poor Father Macaffery come in, please. It's great to see you, Father. I'm sorry about this rude little fleabag of mine."

Father Joe wasn't fooled by her show of mock disdain. He knew just how much Giselle loved the little cat, which had turned up three days after Eve had died. Since then, she told people that it was "just like Eve" to send her a pesky cat for company. The lady had wheeled herself and bug into the kitchen, and Father Joe had followed.

He had never felt ill-at-ease in Giselle's presence before, but today guilt was weighing him down. Giselle seemed nothing but glad to see him.

"Giselle, I've come to apologise. I am so sorry I forgot your groceries."

"It's all right, Father. Max was kind of enough to bring them to me."

"I suppose you know that the scope of my duties has changed somewhat over the last couple of months. Nevertheless, you shouldn't forget your friends, and I did just that. I'm sorry." He stood there in her kitchen awkwardly, looking uncommonly shy.

Giselle looked at him kindly. "Father, you look all tied up in knots. I'm sorry for it. Yes, I was surprised you forgot, but it didn't distress me. You're a busy man. Anyway, believe it or not, this old dame can still organise her own dinner. It's your conversation that I like, and of course, putting you in checkmate."

"I'm sorry though—"

"Relax, Father." She cut him off. "I've forgiven you, God has forgiven you, now you do likewise, please. The most important thing is that you're here now. That's all that matters. Now take a seat and stop worrying."

Father Joe was immensely relieved. He felt a rush of affection for the old woman. "I'd be happy to give you a game now, Giselle, although I know, I don't pose much of a challenge."

"Ah yes, chess is one of my great loves. Chess and Mozart! Eve used to say one should always accompany the other, but then, she was given to a certain dramatic exuberance. But, no sir, I would prefer to talk. I know this is something we haven't talked about until now, but since I have Bindaree's very own heretic in my kitchen. I have been dying to ask about your school in the church. Would you mind, Father?"

Father Joe realised she had disarmed him, no doubt with the intention of extracting this information. He felt himself tense; it seemed almost a habit these days. "I don't mind at all, Giselle. Believe me, my actions in schooling some of Bindaree's less fortunate children—"

"Excuse me, Father," Giselle interrupted. "They are all Indigenous children, is that right?"

"Yes, that's correct. I have alienated a lot of Bindaree society, which was never my goal. The truth is that the handful of children I teach would have had no chance at a proper education if I had not created the school. Mayor Samuels came to see me just this morning, as a matter of fact, to tell me he intends on shutting me down. He seems to have taken the school as a personal affront, and you might as well know he is in the majority."

Giselle's eyes remained fixed on his, but her face betrayed no clue as to how she felt. "And are you going to let him shut you down, Father?" She wheeled over to the kitchen bench and set the electric kettle on to boil.

"No, Ma'am. I can't let my kids down. I won't. That's your answer."

"Bravo, Father! I think it's utterly marvellous!"

Father Joe, these days always ready to defend his actions, was surprised. "You do? I mean the situation isn't perfect, I know that. Having to apologise to you today has made me conscious of the time I'm not spending with some of my other parishioners.

Some of them have made their feelings on the matter abundantly clear, believe me."

"Ah yes, the brick!"

He supposed he should stop being surprised. "You know about that?"

Giselle's laugh was honey-warm and vital. She began to wheel about the kitchen, like a dervish, as they talked. Placing a plate of warm cinnamon rolls on the table in front of him, she said, "Good lord, Father! Everyone knows. The telephone lines have been fairly strumming with gossip. Even an old lady like me can rely on being filled in by some nosey parker. In this instance, my next-door neighbour Mrs Bains couldn't wait to fill me in on everything, she thought she knew. She's a kind soul, Father, but she lives to tattle on others. No, I have been waiting to hear the particulars from you."

"There is a lot of ill feeling in the white community, Giselle. The question of race relations has been seething in Bindaree for decades. The school is only an excuse to vent feelings that have always been there."

"I suspect you're right about that. But tell me, are your children doing well?"

It felt good to laugh. "That's the crazy thing, Giselle." He smiled. "They're doing wonderfully. I'm so proud of them. Kids who never picked up a book before are running to the library after class. We even had a fairly successful game of soccer against The Potter School last week. I can see from my kids' behaviour what this community could be like—if only the adults tried half as hard."

Giselle brought a warm teapot to the table and ladled sugar into one of the cups. "I hope this doesn't sound too condescending, but I'm proud of you, Father! What you're doing, bucking the system, it's a hard thing to do."

"I'm sorry to admit I came here with my armour on. I wasn't sure if you held the same opinion as most every other white person in town. Please forgive me for that."

Giselle's expression was kind. "I'm not offended, Father. Although now might be a good time for you to learn that I'm Jewish."

Father Joe nearly choked on his tea. "You're what?"

"Dresner is a Jewish name. My parents were both teachers at Krakow University, in Poland. With the German invasion came the slurs. Jews are dirty. Jews are thieves. First, my parents were thrown out of the university. Then we were thrown out of our apartment, where we lived with my maternal grandmother. We were sent to Auschwitz. Do you know much about Auschwitz, Father Macaffery?"

Father Joe seemed to have forgotten his tea cooling on the table. He had never met anyone who had survived a concentration camp before. "Only what I've read over the years and what I saw in *Schindler's List*. It's not much, compared to someone who was there, I'm sorry."

"No need to apologise, Father. Auschwitz is hard for anyone to comprehend. I was lucky, I survived, but I always carry it with me. I spent years of my life being told I wasn't even a human being, by ignorant, crazed men. After I was liberated, I resolved to fight bullies wherever I found them." She sipped at her tea and then reached across and patted his hand. "I'm glad I have a friend who is fighting the good fight too."

Father Joe found her gaze penetrating. "You never said anything."

"What? That I'm Jewish? Here, in this country, it never seemed as important. You might say I'm a lapsed Jew, if there is such a thing." She nodded to a framed photograph of Eve that sat on the sideboard. "It seems Jews have one thing in common with Catholics: they both hate homosexuals. I don't mind much anymore, Father. It used to hurt me when I was a young woman. Eventually, I decided I wouldn't give anyone that sort of power over me. Don't think I don't know what this town says about me behind my back. They laughed at Eve and me. Only made me pick my friends more wisely. So, you see, Father, I can't imagine what a black person goes through, because I'm not black, but I can tell you what it feels like to be ostracised, marginalised, made fun of. There are probably a lot of Indigenous issues I wouldn't know squat about, but I feel much better knowing someone like you is in their corner, and believe me, so do they."

Giselle's eyes were moist now, so the Father gave her his hankie, pressing it into her palm. *Remarkable,* he thought. *All this time and until today, I didn't really know her.* "Well, at least I know why you never take communion," he said.

Patting her eyes with the handkerchief, Giselle laughed. "Don't take it personally, Father. You got a dud with me. I just go sometimes for the company, and because you look so handsome in your clerical robes."

"Now I know you're teasing me. Say, if you wouldn't mind, I think I have time for a game of chess with my Jewish homosexual friend."

She leaned over and put her hand on top of his. "Oh, Father Macaffery, you are a flirt. I'd be delighted."

★   ★   ★

Ma Bess wasn't surprised to see Father Joe pull up outside her van on a school day. She'd been expecting this visit ever since the game on Thursday. Gunther wasn't with him, so she supposed the boy was keeping the classroom from disintegrating into anarchy, or that the Father didn't want him along on this particular mission. She sighed heavily as she watched him park.

"Can't stay away from me, can you?" she called out as he approached.

"Hello, Ma. How's my favourite lady?"

"It's my gorgeous body, ain't it? Be truthful now, you wouldn't want the big boss striking you dead!"

"You're a breath of fresh air, Ma. I could never do what I'm doing without your help. I hope you know that."

Taking a seat in the doorway of her van, she raised an eyebrow. "Oh, I think you'd find a way to get your business done, Joe. What concerns me, weighs on me heavy, matter of fact, is what your business is today?"

He stood square and stared right back at her. "Chip Roberts," he said finally.

Ma fetched another sigh. "You don't want to go there, Joe. That path's too dark and twisted, and interfering won't do you, or anyone else, any good."

"He's using his son as a punching bag."

"Maybe. But you're wrong to interfere."

Father Joe couldn't believe his ears. "Don't tell me Ma Bess is scared of a bully?"

Ma Bess stumbled quickly to her feet and stabbed him in the chest with her finger. "I'm not scared of anybody or anything, Preacher. Get that straight! I simply know the consequences of the path you're wandering down in all your well-intentioned naivety."

Father Joe backed up a little and took a seat on the bonnet of his Ford. "Well then, why don't you enlighten me?" He never took his eyes off Ma's.

She looked tired, he realised, and stressed as well, but he couldn't understand how she could turn her back on a situation as grave as this one.

"OK, Joe. If you truly want to know, you'd better come in and hunker down. I'm going to give you a short lesson in blackfella law. You see, if left to your own devices, you would go down there to Chip Robert's place and most likely he'd be in his cups already. You'd tell him he mustn't hit his boy or you'll go back to your ivory tower—"

"I don't have a bloody ivory tower, Ma!"

"It's figurative, Preacher. Listen up. Back in your ivory tower, you phone Child Protective Services. Chip will tell you that his family is none of your business; either that, or he'll just try to kill you. You get pissed off, or *righteous* I think your kind call it. You're looking out for the interests of the boy, after all. You'll call CPS because you're a decent, Christian man. They'll send someone out here to meet with Chip and Sue, and then they'll go back to their air-conditioned offices, and say, 'Yes. Hell, yes. That boy can't stay in that environment one more day.' The police will come, and CPS will drag a boy who probably doesn't want to leave his home, out of there. Then, they're going to say to themselves, 'Shit, what do we do with this kid now?'"

Father Joe thought he already knew the answer. "He could be placed with another family, fostered out . . ."

Ma frowned at him. "Don't interrupt me, please Preacher. The problem they're going to come up against is that boy's colour. Believe me, Joe. It's all about colour. Nobody is going to want a fifteen-year-old Aboriginal boy from The Res. So they'll stick him in some institution, like Tenderwood, until he's eighteen and can care for his own self. Tenderwood is just a prison with flowerbeds. That boy is going to learn a lot of the wrong things in there, and when he turns eighteen, he'll leave that institution. Won't be long before he ends up in another— probably Marsden Prison, your friend Victor Dumagee's old university. He'll learn to thrive in that environment, or to die. Now, you ask yourself Joe, if that isn't your God's honest truth?"

Ma looked at him with a mixture of pity and resignation, an expression far removed from her usual proud countenance.

Father Joe searched his brain for an alternate outcome, but kept coming up blank. Ma was right, as she so often was. It was a torment to him. "So, you're asking me to do nothing?"

Ma reached out and took his hand. "I'm telling you that this little act of charity you're thinking about could cripple poor Doyle Roberts for life. I realise you don't know any other way. You're not a bad person, and you're not a stupid person, Joe. What you are, is a white person."

Her expression was kind, but Father Joe felt as if he had just been slapped in the face. He let go of her hand.

"This is white country, Joe! White people bought it with bullets and liquor and taxes. Since the white settlers arrived, in every exchange between your race and mine, the whites have had the upper hand. Aborigines have become second-class citizens in their own land. You know that book you were reading to the kiddies, *The Chant of Jimmy Blacksmith?*" She saw his eyes widen and hers reciprocated, with amusement. "What? You didn't think I could read? I wanted to know what our kids were learnin'. Anyway, I read it, and I'm sorry to tell you but we haven't advanced much since then. I can see how much you want to make it better for us, especially kiddies like young Doyle. You're a good man, Joe. There are just some things you'll never truly understand about our people. I want it to be better too, believe me. But it took us a long time to get this fucked up, and it'll take us a long time to fix it. I, myself, cannot conceive of a time when black and whites will be equal. Do you understand? As hard as I try, I just can't conceive of that."

Suddenly, Ma laughed heartily, which didn't seem appropriate, given the conversation. "Do you want to know something, Joe? And this will split you in half. My great-grandfather was white. I don't share that with many people, but I'm a slice of Irish, just like you. Now, please. I want you to leave this situation with Chip to me. You can't fix it your way, and I think you know that now."

Father Joe shook his head sadly. He felt awfully weary. "It goes against all my principles, Ma. I'll let you deal with it in your own way, but if I see any more injuries on Doyle, I'll go there and bless Chip Roberts with a right hook."

She nodded and took his hand again. "Just you leave it with me, Joe. I still have a little respect among my people."

Father Joe squeezed her hand. "You're one of God's angels, Ma. I'm certain of it."

"Funny bloody excuse for an angel. You sure, you're not hitting the booze?"

"If I were, Ma, I'd only drink with a fellow Irishman."

She snorted at him and got to her feet. "OK, stop suckin' up my oxygen, Preacher, and don't let the door hit you on the way out. I've got business to attend to."

★ ★ ★

The weekends were beginning to feel lonely without the kids, especially given the hostility coming from members of his congregation. Nigel Tomlinson had made good on his promise and had not stepped back inside the little church. Seeing a *No Blacks* sign in the window of a local restaurant on Sunday did nothing to improve his mood.

On Monday morning, the class bombshell was that the young Lothario, Doyle, had somehow managed to woo shy Lilly. Their budding romance was responsible for a general upheaval in seating arrangements. Doyle now insisted on sitting next to his girl. Father Joe noted that Tommy King looked a little lost. Father Joe hoped Lilly's association with Doyle might draw her out of herself. She was still painfully shy, and Doyle was anything but.

"OK, troops. Listen up. I need two things from you today. I know it's Monday, but I need your attention on the assignment I am about to give you, and I need your parents to sign a permission slip so that we can all go on a little field trip."

Mudguard stopped rapping on the desktop with his ruler. The others, whose attention had been tweaked, stopped talking and faced him.

"What trip, Father?" asked Doyle, grinning ridiculously.

"With your parent's permission, we are going to Marsden to attend Career's Day. I need you to be dressed nicely. And yes, that means you have to wear shoes, guys. Doyle Roberts, I don't want to see the band of your underwear riding outside your pants. Do you understand me? All of you will be representing our school, and it will be judged on your behaviour. This means you will be polite and respectful, got it?"

"Sounds OK, Father," agreed Mudguard. "I reckon we can do that."

"Father, what if our parents don't sign?" asked Jessica.

"If that's the case, and I'll be sorry if it is, you can't come. I need their permission. And don't think you can sign the slip yourself, because I can sniff a bit of blarney from a mile away. You have to remember, I'm Irish, and we're superior human beings."

"Yeah, right and I'm yellow," said Doyle.

He let them talk it out for a moment. They seemed excited by the prospect, and he knew that some of them had never been out of Bindaree. When Mike had told him about Career's Day, he had decided on the spot. The seniors should be starting to toss career ideas around. He wanted his kids to have rosy futures, not to settle for a feckless existence in The Res, anticipating their next dole payment.

Gunther raised his hand.

"Yes son, what is it?"

"You said *two* things, Father. What's the second thing?"

"Good of you to ask. We have an assignment to do on the book we just finished. *The Outsiders.*"

There was a chorus of groans, but they were less than heartfelt. The book Father Joe had selected for them this time, a book about a teenage gang war between the rich and poor, had excited them all. It wasn't surprising they could identify with the characters.

"Listen up. This is what I want from you: I want the juniors to write a letter, as their favourite character, to that character's parents. One full page, please. Seniors, I want a written essay on the lack of parents or adults in general throughout the book. I want you really exercising your brains, guys. What's the author saying? Why are the adult figures glimpsed so briefly, if at all? I want two pages from seniors. It should take you until after lunch. If we have enough time, after you're done, we can head down to the beach for some cricket practice. Maybe I'll actually manage to hit one of Jessica's balls. Before you get started, can someone tell me where Freddy Fingers is today?"

"Doin' stuff," said Tommy sullenly.

Father Joe sighed. "OK, I'll talk to him when he comes back. In the meantime, Doyle could you write down the assignment for Freddy and give it to him, please. He also needs to get his parents' permission to come to Career's Day, unless he's 'doin' stuff' on that day too."

It frustrated Father Joe when one of his kids seemed to be going backwards. There was always going to be one kid who didn't take learning seriously, and he feared that lollygagging Freddy Fingers was that kid. Well, Freddy would discover just how stubborn an Irishman Father Joe could be.

"Gunther, could I talk to you outside for a minute?"

Gunther jumped out of his seat. When they were outside, he asked, "What's up, Father?"

"I just wanted to ask after your folks, son. I see you each Sunday, but I haven't seen your folks for a couple of weeks now. Everything all right?"

Pain creased the boy's normally smiling face. "They've been copping some flack, Father. There aren't that many Abos in church, you know? They feel a bit like flies in milk. Anyway, they said that they can pray anywhere. They think the school is more important than attending church at the moment. I'm sorry, Father."

Father Joe put his hand on the boy's shoulder. "It's all right, son. They've done nothing wrong. I'm sorry they don't feel comfortable in church, but your folks are decent people, please give them my love, and tell them my door is always open to them."

"I will, Father."

"OK, now go get stuck into that assignment, and make it good."

"Yes, Father."

Back inside, he looked at his class of misfits, their heads bent over their papers, and sent up a prayer of thanks to the boss. Despite the toxic attitude of many in their community, his kids were thriving. When he was with them like this, that anyone took issue with what he was trying to do seemed ludicrous to him. He prayed for the tolerance his kids seemed to naturally possess so he could deal with the contrary adults that surrounded them. There had been many moments when the Father had questioned the wisdom of what he was doing to the community, but then he had only to think of Giselle Dresner's story or Ma Bess's bawdy, irreverent wisdom, and he was set straight on his path once more. What he said to Ma was correct: God had sent him some angels to guide him over the rocky path—and what a wonderful, ragtag bunch they were. But what really kept him on track were the kids. Of course, he wished he could help more. He still saw kids Gunther's age prowling The Res on his weekly visits, obviously not in school, and floundering for direction. He told himself that if God had wanted him to help more, then more would have come. He looked at them scribbling away furiously, or in Mudguard's case, gazing out the window. This classroom was his ark, and like Noah, he only got a select few to influence. *This is God's will,* he told himself, *and it will have to be enough.*

★   ★   ★

That night, alone in the presbytery, once he had finally pushed Gunther out the door, Father Joe read through the essays the kids had turned in. There were a couple of clumsy efforts from the juniors, but the kids had mostly captured the spirit of the book and the essays showed an analysis and depth that belied their years. The reason they had loved the book, he knew, was because they were outsiders too. He looked at Gunther's essay.

> *Adults are absent from the story because the author wanted to show how kids would cope with the world without adults making up all the rules.*

And this from Tommy:

> *The writer wanted to show the loyalty kids have for each other. Also, that childhood is a magical time, that's gone too quickly.*

Father Joe was deeply moved by the kids' explanations. In a lot of ways, his kids were wiser than the adults around them. Reading Tommy's piece, he wondered how magical the angry young man's life had been up until now. There wasn't much magic to be found in The Res, yet he persisted with the idea that magic existed somewhere, and that children were the beneficiaries of it. In this regard, Father Joe applauded the boy's stubbornness.

CHAPTER 6

On the day they got their assignments back, there was no mirth on the face of Doyle Roberts. He was royally pissed off.

"Father, I've got to talk to you, outside."

"No problem, lad."

The rest of the class watched the steadily growing thundercloud of Doyle's expression as the two of them walked outside.

"OK, Father, how come you gave me a 'D' for that work? That was a great book, and I told you what I thought of it. You've made me look real stupid, Father."

"I know you liked the book, Doyle. You told me several times. But whether you liked it or not isn't the question. How much attention were you paying when I handed out the assignment?"

"I paid good attention, Father."

Father Joe pointed to the offending paper, to a passage written in Doyle's nearly illegible scrawl. "Doyle, you wrote here: 'the guy who wrote *The Outsiders* was a good bloke who didn't like grown-ups.' This is work way below the standard I expect of you. It doesn't sound as if you gave my essay question any thought at all."

"Bullshit, Father!"

The smile left the priest's face momentarily. "Don't curse at me, boy. It doesn't make you sound any smarter. If you had been paying attention when we discussed the book, you would know *The Outsiders* was written by a teenage girl, Susan Eloise Hinton, not some 'good bloke.'"

Doyle's face told Father Joe what the priest had expected—that he was indeed receiving this news for the first time.

"A girl wrote it?"

"Yes. A girl who probably paid attention in class. This might not seem particularly fair, but I marked you down because I know you are capable of a lot better. I need you to use your brain, Doyle. In this school, if you are lazy, you get a lazy grade."

The boy's tough expression faltered. "Yeah, but Father, Lilly's going to think I'm stupid now."

"I don't think she'll think that, Doyle, but you could show her that you've got some smarts. We both know that you do."

"Could I do it again, Father? Make it better?" pleaded the boy.

"Absolutely. Just remember that when you get out into the big bad world, there aren't any do-overs."

"I know. It sucks! Do you think I could ever write a book like that, Father?"

"That's just it, Doyle, I think you could do just about anything you set your mind to."

The boy was smiling now. "I think I'd rather bat for Australia."

"OK, Donald Bradman. Let's get inside before Mudguard tries to stage a coup."

The next morning, Doyle, looking exceptionally pleased with himself, presented Father Joe with a much more thoughtful work, if still written in the same daunting script.

The next week continued to be a testament to teenage love. Father Joe began to think the only thing that could separate Doyle and Lilly was a bucket of cold water. In class, the girl was still extremely reserved around Father Joe and her classmates. He had no idea how Doyle had penetrated her armour. He had to admit, though, that Lilly seemed as crazy about Doyle as he was about her, and he felt glad when he saw the shy smile flit across her face. It was the maintenance of that smile that prompted his next awkward conversation with Doyle.

He caught up with the boy at lunchtime in the parking lot. "Can I have a word, Doyle?"

"Am I in trouble, Father?"

Not yet, and I'm hoping to cut any off at the pass, kiddo. "No, I wanted to have a word to you about Lilly."

At the mention of her name, Doyle's whole demeanour changed. He looked as if someone had turned the light on inside.

He's got it bad all right, thought Father Joe.

"What about her, Father."

"Doyle, you two look great together. I'm glad you found someone like Lilly. I think she's very good for you, but lad, I don't want you busting into her life chock-full of trouble and testosterone, and screwing it up. On the first day of school I told you all that we have to respect each other. That includes respect for your classmates too."

The boy's frown furrowed his forehead. He raised his hand, palm first. "Father, if you're thinking of talking to me about sex, you can forget it. It ain't happening."

"All I'm saying, Doyle, is that girls like Lilly are rare, and they command respect. She was in real danger at The Potter School, so we accepted her here. But in accepting her into this school, we've effectively told her she's protected here, that this is a safe place for her. Now, you're absolutely right, you haven't done anything wrong—yet—but that girl has placed her trust in you. Don't let it be misplaced because you can't control yourself. That's it. That's all I've got to say. I hope you understand why I felt I had to say something." Father Joe was glad the discussion was finished. Doyle was nearly purple with embarrassment, so Father Joe hoped what he told the boy had sunk in. He liked Lilly; he didn't want to see her hurt.

Doyle looked at him with a benign expression and shrugged. "You might like Lilly, Father. The thing is, I love her. I won't hurt her, I promise."

★   ★   ★

The class was scheduled to leave for Marsden on Friday. Although he had told the kids he absolutely required their parents' permission, by Wednesday he had just five signed permission slips out of nineteen. Mudguard's mother had even actually referred to him by his bizarre nickname, he noted with a laugh. But for the others, once again he would need Ma Bess's help.

It was a hot, sultry morning when he rolled into The Res under a cloud of red dust—straight into the midst of a battle. Chip Roberts was standing outside Ma's van yelling at her, and Ma was yelling right back in a lusty, frequently obscene, vibrato. Percy was sitting meekly in Ma's doorway, quietly watching the proceedings with all the verve of a courtroom stenographer. Chip Roberts was drunk again.

"I don't give a fuck, Ma! Who I have stay in my house is my business. Stay out of it," hollered Chip.

"Your own wife won't come back until he's gone, you hear? Don't you think that speaks volumes? Anyway, I'm not telling you where she's at."

"I'll knock on every fuckin' door in The Res until I find the bitch."

Father Joe didn't want to get into the middle of whatever was going on, but when Chip spotted him it only served to enrage him further. "We'll, looky here, it's the bloody Father."

"Hello, Mr Roberts."

"At least I know where I can find my son, don't I? He's off pretending he's fuckin' Shakespeare with you, you bastard."

Father Joe didn't rise to the bait. He knew from experience that arguing with a drunk was foolhardy. "Doyle's a bright boy. You should be very proud of him."

"Don't fuckin' tell me about my son. His mother might believe your bullshit, but I tell you there's no way you're taking him out of Bindaree for some goddamn circle jerk, and that's a fact."

Ma reached her limit. "Chip, go the hell home! You're trying my patience," she said.

"I'm leaving now, but I'll find her, Ma," said Chip, determined to get the last word. "No bloody woman tells me who I can and can't have in my own home." He turned and wandered back down towards his house, nearly falling over half a dozen times along the way.

Percy stood up quickly and let Ma take up her familiar position in the doorway. She was perspiring and breathing hard, and utterly magnificent to see. "I'm sorry about that, Joe. You pick your moments, don't you?"

"Are you all right, Ma?" he asked.

"Oh yeah. I'll be fine. Percy, could you get me a beer, please? I'm parched from all that toin' and froin'."

When Percy slipped inside momentarily, Father Joe asked, "Have Doyle and his mother really moved out?"

"The boy hasn't said anything to you?"

"Not a word." The admission stung him.

"Sue and Doyle have been staying at Alice King's for the past few days. Chip came home last week with Victor Dumagee in tow. He's sleeping on their goddamn lounge."

Alarm coursed through Father Joe. He couldn't abide the thought of a jackal like Victor anywhere near one of his kids. "Can't we do anything?"

"You mean can we make him leave? Not really. As Chip said, it's his house. The stubborn bastard will keep him there just to spite me."

"What if we told the police where they could find him? He's packing a handgun."

Percy handed Ma a cold beer and snorted. Ma gave him an appraising look and then nodded toward him. "He's right, Joe. Victor's too smart to hand them the evidence they need against him. Besides, as you already know, the coppers aren't busting a gut to come in here."

"That man is bad trouble, Ma," he said.

"Aren't you supposed to love all men, good and bad?"

"God loves everyone, Ma. I'm just a man. I don't for a minute claim to have my Lord's love and forgiveness."

Ma smiled at him. "You're a good man for a preacher, Joe. Bloody bull headed at times, but a good man nonetheless. You love those kiddies, I know that."

"I do, and I love you too," said Father Joe.

"Of course you do. What's not to love?" She shimmied in the dust.

Percy and Father Joe laughed in unison, until Percy gave the preacher a quick glance and stopped as quickly as he started.

Ma smiled at them both before chugging the rest of her beer. She looked over towards the Robert's house. Victor Dumagee had come out onto the porch and was smirking at them. Ma frowned at his sheer audacity. "We've got to get him gone, Joe. That man's a diseased mongrel, if I ever saw one. I know what you said to Jeremy, but I'm as worried for you as I am for the kiddies, as long as that man stays here. Just be careful, please."

"I will be, Ma."

Ten minutes later, after asking Ma's help with the permission slips, Father Joe drove out of The Res and back to his students. He stared at Doyle as he entered the church. He didn't seem any different, but Father Joe dwelt on the situation for the rest of the day.

CHAPTER 7

Four months after the establishment of St Bernadette's church school, the kids were thriving but the town of Bindaree was festering. The streets were clean, the lawns manicured, the yachts and trawlers sailed serenely off Saxton Head. Everything on the outside maintained its sublime image, but inside the houses and pubs, vicious words and rumours sliced the air. Opinion was rife, with spouse pitted against spouse, and neighbour against neighbour. Any harmony remembered seemed to be a vixen of questionable morals.

The mayor received many a letter (and a good deal of unsolicited advice) on how to rid Bindaree of the black scourge. To his credit, he did not consider some of the more extreme ideas. Grady Samuels was a public servant who abided by the laws of the day. He didn't like getting any dirt, or ink, under his fingernails, particularly any that might came back to stain him politically later on. No matter his personal beliefs, he was a careful captain of the image he wished for Bindaree. He had already talked with Sergeant Morcom of the Bindaree police—a robust doofus of a man, who, in Grady's estimation, would have trouble reciting the alphabet. Morcom had told him the black school was a sound legal concern. Samuels felt stifled by laws that favoured the whacko priest, and he resented the developing notion among the townsfolk that he was being lax and ineffectual. Then he heard that the black students were going to Marsden, to a Career's Day. Marsden was Bindaree's nearest neighbour, and five times its size. Samuels had always fought to have Bindaree recognized as the town as more than just a small rural hamlet, because Bindaree counted on Marsden residents' tourism dollars. Marsden was inland and was not possessed of the beautiful coastline that bordered most of Bindaree. The last thing Grady needed was a group of little black sambos fouling up the image of his town. Unfortunately, they were travelling with Mike Potter, the senile old fool, so he was unable to prevent them from going. Grady reached into his desk drawer and withdrew some Aspirin and some antacid. It seemed that ever since Father Joe Macaffery came to town, Grady Samuels had had nothing but headaches.

★   ★   ★

Excitement over the Marsden trip was diluted by the knowledge they would be sharing a coach with seniors from The Potter School. With the exception of the soccer game, the black and white students hadn't been in such proximity in months. Father Joe had appealed to his kids not to get riled by any taunts, and it seemed they listened. Still, Father Joe was disappointed that two of his students were missing out. He had received no explanation for why Jessica was not permitted to go, and Chip Roberts had made good on his word and refused to let Doyle attend. However, Doyle had come in to town to see Lilly on to the bus, and the two were acting out a goodbye scene worthy of a Hollywood tearjerker.

"OK guys, enough sucking face already. We'll be back this afternoon, and you can kiss her again then, Romeo. On the bus, Lilly."

"Yes, Father."

Doyle unwrapped himself from the slip of a girl and asked Father Joe, "Will you take care of her for me, Father?"

"You have my word, Doyle. I'm just sorry you won't be joining us."

Doyle shrugged hopelessly. "Yeah well, I should have known he wouldn't let me go. It's not really a surprise."

"We'll tell you all about it. What are you planning on doing this morning?"

"I thought I might go over to the library and work on our new assignment. I could stir up Miss Walpole a bit."

"Just don't go cheating on Lilly with her."

"Father! The woman has only one eyebrow!"

The ride to Marsden was uneventful, even with the undercurrent of tension that was ever present between black and white. There was some rankling about the soccer game, but it seemed good-natured enough. On the way there, Mike Potter told Father Joe he had instituted a strict NO BULLYING policy at his school. When asked about it, the kids were for the most part positive and thoughtful. He said he could one day see a successfully blended school. At least, that was what he was striving for. Father Joe was grateful for all of his efforts. When the coach pulled up in front of the Marsden Conventional Centre, he let The Potter School kids off first and then turned to the thirteen shining black faces of St Bernadette's School.

"What's the matter, Father?" asked Mudguard.

"Nothing, I want you to enjoy yourselves this afternoon. Ask questions if you want, but I expect you to be polite to everyone you talk to. Am I understood? We'll meet back here at three."

"Father, you've got to learn to relax," said Mudguard gravely. "We've got this."

"All right then, troops. Go, ask, and learn. Tommy, if you see any literature or pamphlets you think Doyle might be interested in, can you gather some please?"

While the rest of the kids raced for the door, both Gunther and Lilly hung back to find out which way Father Joe was headed.

"If you don't mind, could we walk with you a bit, Father?"

"Absolutely, as long as you don't mind strolling with a geriatric."

Lilly's laugh had a tinkling musical quality. The only time he had heard it previously was when she was listening to one of Doyle's tall tales. He took it as a sign she was coming out of her shell.

Father Joe was impressed by the breadth and diversity of the displays. One from the Australian Defence Force Academy (ADFA) had a reasonable crowd around it. There were booths for different trades and apprenticeships, as well as teaching, police, the SES, and a stall that gave information about further education as a prerequisite for entering certain professions.

Gunther and Lilly were walking next to him, deep in conversation.

"Nursing school? That's great, Lilly. You'd make an excellent nurse. We better go over to the TAFE booth and see what you'll need for a nursing certificate," suggested Gunther.

"What about you? Don't you want to have a look around?"

"I don't need to. I'm going to the seminary. I'm going to be a priest, like the Father," said Gunther quietly.

"You're still decided on that then?" asked Father Joe.

"Yep, God decided for me, I guess."

Father Joe smiled at him, but Gunther was looked at Lilly. "Don't tell the others yet, Lilly, please. They'll just rag on me about it, and it's not a joke."

"I won't say anything, Gunny." The girl took Gunther's hand and squeezed it.

Father Joe looked up at that moment to see Tommy King, with a crunched brow, staring at the place where Lilly and Gunther's hands met. He hoped the boy wasn't getting the wrong impression. An alarm bell rang in his head, but it was silenced when the two kids wandered off to see about the requirements for Lilly's nursing certificate.

Father Joe strolled around, keeping an eye on his kids, for the rest of the afternoon. When trouble eventually erupted, he told himself that, had he been a smarter man, he would have anticipated and smothered it earlier, while it was only a spark. He found Tommy King yelling threats at one of the boys from The Potter's School—Phillip something or other—and at a uniformed man catering to those who wished to know more about the armed forces. The man looked decidedly nonplussed at the situation that had flared up in his midst.

Father Joe hoped the camaraderie between Gunther and Lilly hadn't set him off. The cause of Tommy's newest indignity seemed to be the podgy, myopic boy Phillip whatshisname. Tommy hadn't hit the kid yet, but the volume with which he was ripping into him—even with the young army captain frantically trying to diffuse the situation—suggested it wouldn't be long before he threw a haymaker at the little snot. Father Joe only thanked the boss that he got there in time to save the white boy's dental work.

"Tommy, come with me. Right now, young man!"

"Father, did you hear what this shithead said to me?"

"Tommy, mind your language. I want to see you out in the coach. Right now!"

Tommy's barometer had not yet returned to normal. He let out a stream of curses as he followed Father Joe obediently outside. "But Father, did you hear what he said?"

"We're going to talk about it in the coach."

Tommy picked up each foot as if it weighed the same as a bag of spuds. The defiant young teenager Father Joe had first met in the hospital was back. When he started going off again, Father Joe told him to shut up so vehemently that the boy sat in slack-jawed surprise.

"I'm going to tell you something I should have told you the first day I taught you. Listen up Tommy, so that you can repeat this to the others one day. But first, what does the word 'expectation' mean?"

The boy looked at him as though he had at last done the expected thing and turned traitor on them. "It's when someone believes something about you," he answered sullenly.

"That's as clear an explanation as we need for my purposes. We're going to talk about expectations. Out there," he waved outside the coach, "and home in Bindaree, they have a belief, or in some cases just a strong hope, that you are going to fail. That is their expectation of you, Tommy. They don't think you need an education, because they don't think you'll ever make anything of your life."

He could see the boy was still fuming, but at least he had his attention now. "Now, I have an expectation of you too. My expectation is that you will turn up. You will listen to what I tell you before you dismiss it as white man's voodoo. And you will try your best. But the expectations you have to live up to are the ones you have for yourself. For a boy who didn't want a bar of school, you've turned in some particularly insightful work, but it seems to me that you don't expect enough of yourself. A man with any self-respect wouldn't have gone off his head at that little chump. He would have laughed at him. Tommy, I want you and the others to chart the course of your own lives, not fall into some stereotype of what others believe of you. That's part of why we're here today. Do you understand?"

The scowl lifted slowly from the boy's face, and he nodded.

"I have to hope that your expectations of yourself are a lot higher than getting into it with some half-wit. Otherwise, Tommy my lad, you're aiming far too low, and I'm not doing my job properly."

"Do you want to know why I got so mad?"

"Only if you feel you have to tell me, and only with the understanding that you are going back out there to apologise for your behaviour, both to the soldier and to that little twit."

Tommy nodded. He no longer looked angry, just embarrassed and tired.

Too tired for a person of his age, thought Father Joe.

"Promise you won't laugh?"

"I won't laugh at you, boy."

"I want to join the army. I thought I'd find out what I had to do to join up. Phillip said they don't take Abos 'cause we're too stupid to pass the exam."

Father Joe sighed and sat down opposite the boy. "Stupid little shit!"

"Father!"

"Not you, Tommy. Phillip Whosit, with the Coke-bottle glasses. He's a stupid little shit, and he's ignorant." Father Joe could finally see the acceptance of him in the boy's eyes.

"Have you given this a lot of thought, Tommy? Because it's a big commitment? What do your folks say?"

"I've been thinking about it for a while now. My dad hasn't said yes, but my mum thinks it could be a good thing for me. At least it's a way out of The Res."

Despite the fact that Australia was involved in conflict overseas, Father Joe agreed that Tommy King might find camaraderie and discipline in one of the forces, which he certainly wouldn't get staying in The Res.

"We've never talked about the night Trey was attacked, have we? Please tell me the boy sitting before me now is not the same boy who cut and ran on his little brother?"

Tommy looked wounded by the memory of that night and that the Father had finally brought it up.

"He's not, Father. I wouldn't do that again."

"Then I'll tell you what, if you come back with me and apologise to 'the little shit' and to the poor bloody soldier, and you make it sincere"—he gave Tommy a fiercely proud look— "and that means don't roll your eyes at me, then you and I will have a chat with the soldier about what you'll need to get into ADFA."

He held out his hand to the boy. "Deal?"

"Deal!"

In the end, there was no bloodshed. To his credit, Tommy's apology sounded suitably sincere, although the precious Mr Phillip Goldman did not receive it with the same grace with which it was offered. He seemed to be about to launch into an indignant tirade, when Mike Potter clamped his hand down on the boy's shoulder and told him he didn't want to hear anything else out of him for the rest of the trip.

The kids were all back at the coach at three-o-clock, except for Gunther and Lilly, who it seemed were taking a detour via Paris, France. Twenty minutes later, they raced up to the coach, hand in hand. Lilly was clutching a bunch of pamphlets.

"Sorry, Father," said Gunther. "We lost track of time."

"Gunther, my boy, I'm sure, if I tried hard enough I could work up some reasonable-sized irritation at both of you, but to be totally honest, I'm just too bloody tired. Get in."

With that, the coach headed back to Bindaree, where the real troubles of their existence were threatening to greet them.

★   ★   ★

Father Joe also later chastised himself for not having predicted Monday's schoolyard battle. He should have listened to that internal alarm that had gone off in Marsden, when he had spotted Tommy glaring his disapproval at Gunther and Lilly. It was obvious that, over the course of the weekend, among the tales Doyle had been told about the trip was the perceived disloyalty of his friend and his girl.

By the time Father Joe got to them, Gunther was lying on his back in the car park, his nose bleeding copiously. Doyle was standing over him, fists clenched, with all the misspent fury of Othello.

"You prick! You couldn't wait to take her away from me, could you?" screamed the boy.

Father Joe pushed through the throng of teenagers and seized Doyle by the shoulder. The boy only wriggled out of his grip and raised his fist.

"You want to lower that fist. Right now!" Father Joe bent over to help Gunther to his feet. The boy was a bit wobbly. He had certainly come off second best in the encounter. Lilly was crying and was refusing to take Doyle's hand.

"What happened here?" asked Father Joe.

"Well, Father, it seems like Gunther's gone and done something stupid," said Mudguard, scratching his head, as if it were hard for him to deduce exactly what had happened.

"Thank you, Mudguard. But I wasn't asking you. Everyone, except for Doyle, Gunther and Lilly, inside now."

When the last of the spectators had entered the church, Father Joe turned to Lilly.

"What happened here, Lilly?"

The girl was trembling and still refusing Doyle's attempts to take her hand.

"Tommy told Doyle that Gunther and I hooked up on the Marsden trip, and Doyle hit him. It isn't true," added the girl, now looking into Doyle's furious face. "We're just friends, Father. I'd never do that to Doyle."

"Doyle, do you have anything to say in your defence? Because it doesn't look good, boy."

"They were holding hands. They, I mean Gunther . . . I don't know, Father," spluttered the boy."

"I will tell you now that I didn't see anything in Marsden, besides two friends worrying over the fact that you weren't there with them."

Doyle's shoulders slumped in on themselves. His anger seemed to have morphed into mortification. He turned to Gunther, who was now holding a handkerchief to his nose. "I'm sorry, Gunny. I thought you were trying to steal her away from me."

"I'd never do that, man." Gunther's voice was nasally. He was trying unsuccessfully to staunch the flow of blood. "We're mates. Lilly's a mate too, is all. Father, I've got to go wash off some of this blood."

"Go do that, son. Lilly, you go with him back to class. Doyle, I don't know what to do with you. There are enough people in this town who want to fight this school, without us fighting within it. I want you to take a few minutes to calm down and then I want you to come inside and do some work while I think of what your consequences should be."

The boy nodded and leaned up against the chain link fence.

He found Gunther in the bathroom, stripped to the waist, trying to stem the flow of blood from his nose.

"Tilt your head back and pinch the bridge of your nose."

The boy did as he was told.

"Father, I've gotta wash the blood out of this T-shirt before I get home or my Mum will chuck a spaz!"

Father Joe smiled. "Well, we don't want anyone's mother chucking a spaz, do we? Give it to me."

Father Joe ran it under cold water and worked at the stain with some soap until the shirt was free of bloodstains. "I'll get you one of my T-shirts to put on until this dries. Although, I think from the swelling that your mum is going to know something happened. Perhaps you tripped, hurrying to class?" he suggested.

"Do you really think I should lie to her, Father?"

"What I think, is that maybe you shouldn't alarm her when there's no need."

"I'll think about it." The boy was still looking at him. "Father, why did you start boxing?"

"Because I was young and too arrogant to be part of a team. That's not to say boxing isn't a great discipline. I just did it for all the wrong reasons. What I should do, though, is teach you how to block a punch."

"No offence, Father, but I don't really want to know. Doyle's hurting a lot more than I am at the moment anyway."

Father Joe didn't reply. What could he possibly say? By the end of the day, it was clear that Gunther was right. It was also clear what punishment Doyle would incur. Lilly would not look at or talk to him, despite his many overtures. She had seen a side to her boyfriend that scared her, and it was equally clear she wasn't going to put up with it. Father Joe realised any punishment he imposed would be unnecessary; the boy was already suffering for his crime.

★ ★ ★

With no school, Saturday was usually a time for surfing, reflection and prayer. But by ten in the morning the mercury had hit thirty-four and the ocean was flat, so Father Joe returned to the presbytery to change and then took a stroll down Bindaree's Main Street. He saw more signage up, rejecting blacks in Cameron's Grocery Mart and, even more unbelievably, in the window of The Rose and Crown Tavern. When he walked into the Crown for a quiet beer, the eyes that met his ranged from disinterested to downright hostile. He realised he had been kidding himself in his belief the town's anger was diminishing. He knew Grady Samuels was feeding the white wrath, but he felt tainted by the prevailing attitude. Even the barman, Hank, who despite never gracing a pew at church had always had a ready smile and a kind word for Father Joe on the occasions when he wandered in, seemed not to want to engage him in his usual cheery barman's banter.

Father Joe ordered a schooner and sat quietly, contemplating his new role of outcast. He thought of the stalwart churchgoers who attended St Bernadette's every Sunday, and he wondered what the repercussions for them were. It should have opened his eyes when the Pearces stopped coming. Nothing could stop Gunther, of course, who now viewed it as instruction in his choice of profession. It made Father Joe angry to think of anyone ostracising a boy as gentle and honest as Gunther. That lead him to thinking about the deprivations Giselle Dresner had survived during the Holocaust, and how she had the courage to come through them and create a life out of nothing, without being embittered or capitulating in whom she chose to love. Father Joe ordered another beer from the bar, choosing to ignore the few patrons warming their bar stools. *I may as well be black to them,* he thought. One lesson his father had instilled in him was that a bar room was an excellent place to have a crisis of confidence, and that was what he was suffering. He knew in his heart God wanted him to help his students, but he kept asking himself what he could do to change the mindset of their neighbours. Above all else, he mustn't get angry. Ugly things happened when he got angry. He remembered breezing into town three years ago after speaking at length with Father Passali, pissed off, and stretched tight as a rubber band. He had fallen in love with the little white church on the bluff overlooking the sea. He told himself this was his new start: a place where he could help people and revel in God's handiwork. He had lost everything but his faith in the Lord. The thing he wanted, when he had first arrived in Bindaree, was not to wipe the sin off his hands. Despite what innocents like Gunther believed, Father Joe knew that wasn't possible. What he had wanted was to know how a man shouldered his sins and started anew? Because that was what Bindaree had symbolised for him: a new life. Had he actually been so naïve as to think he could erase the past and start again? When he approached the bar to get another beer, Hank's hands remained motionless on the bar. Father Joe tensed automatically. The barman only looked embarrassed.

"Is there a problem, Hank?"

"Father, you've always struck me as the genuine type, which is why this is hard to tell you, but I seriously think someone should . . ."

"What is it?"

"I think you should know there are some people in town who are calling you 'Joe Coon.'"

Father Joe slowly put his wallet back in his pocket. "Are they really? Well, I'll tell you what, Hank. If any of those people happen into the bar in the next hour, you tell them they can find me over at the YWCA hitting a bag. Maybe they'd like to call me that to my face. I should think you'd be a little more selective in the kind of people you let in here, or is that it, Hank? Is this you being selective? Because, I can always get a cold beer at one of the other dusty throats in town."

"I didn't say *I* called you that, Father."

"No, you didn't, did you? You just listened to the ignorant son of a bitch who did." He slammed out into the afternoon sunlight, blood pounding in his temples. Once more, he was confused by the people around him.

Pounding on the heavy bag at the Y until sweat streamed down his face and arms made him feel only marginally better. A feeling that was dispelled instantly when he looked up and saw Victor Dumagee at the entrance to the men's change room, talking to a young boy who couldn't have been twelve years old.

Father Joe walked over while taking off his gloves. "Hello, Victor. You still here, or have you just stopped by to collect your suitcase?"

The boy stared at both men with confusion.

"Hello, Father. I really do think there's room for both of us, don't you? I mean, I don't see where our two situations get tangled," said Victor.

"Then you must be mentally defective as well as deaf, Victor. I said I want you gone, and I meant it."

Victor just grinned insolently at him. "I'm not sure you're in a position to make that happen."

Father Joe tossed a glove at the man. It hit him in the chest. "Put that on and we'll see."

"Yeah, I heard somewhere that you used to like to swing at people. What happened to 'love they neighbour,' huh?"

"In your case, I'm sure the Lord would let me make an exception.

Victor's grin became a scowl. "Nup, that's not how I do things. When I do you, it will be on my own turf. When I say."

Father Joe nodded at the glove on the ground. "Get out of here, before I pick that up and use it on you."

It was hard to tell if his words had any impact on the thug, but Victor pushed the younger boy out of the doorway like a broom, and followed without saying anything.

Father Joe couldn't work out whether he was relieved or disappointed. One thing he did know: the problem with Victor Dumagee would be resolved sooner rather than later.

The morning's events had him thinking. If everybody had an opinion, and everyone was making his or her opinion known (and it seemed that was indeed the case), then why wasn't he making his? Was it because he felt illegitimate? He shouldn't let his own position affect his kids, if that was indeed what he was doing. It was true he had never used the pulpit for campaigning before. His style of preaching was more friendly reason than the incessant screaming of the hothead evangelists that preached from the television early Sunday mornings. But he had a voice, and up until now he hadn't been using it. He wouldn't be simply arguing for the school and his role in it, he would be sticking up for his kids. He was their voice.

Father Joe decided it was high time he threw a brick of his own.

CHAPTER 8

"Friends, I would like to address an issue that has polarised our community over the past few months. I believe I was given a task by our Lord, which was genius in both its simplicity and its purpose. It was to take some of our Indigenous youth who were not being taught, and to school them here, in the church, myself. Unfortunately, what I did not anticipate was the hostility the school would incite within the wider Bindaree community."

He could see the immediate discomfit of some of his congregation. Mayor Samuels was seated in the front pew, accompanied by his unfortunate wife, Olive, and the man's smug smile taunted him.

"It seems to me that every soul in this town has an opinion as to the Godliness of our task. I say 'our' because, although I am the teacher, I have received great help from some of our residents. They, like me, want nothing more than to show compassion to our neighbours and to lend a helping hand to those who need it."

He leant over the pulpit as he spoke, as if confiding a powerful truth. He hardly noticed his hands resting on the infamous brick. "When I accepted this new task, I was ignorant of a fact that has come back to bite me—that in Bindaree, getting a fair and just education is a matter of colour. Believe me, I have been shocked by the opinions out there, and my students and I have encountered difficulties where there was no need for them. Despite this, my students are thriving. For that, I thank the good Lord, who I believe is shining his face upon our makeshift little classroom."

A couple in one of the front pews stood up and walked briskly out of the church, without comment.

Their departure was all the comment Father Joe needed. He continued, "I wonder, though, at all those who have aligned themselves against us, if only in spirit. Is this not a country, a state, a town, that professes to have a duty of care to all children? Is not the right to a decent education one of the chief pillars we proudly acknowledge holds up our society? Where is it written that an education is only accessible to white children? We are not talking about juvenile delinquents here, or kids run afoul of the law. These are ordinary kids, kids between the ages of ten and sixteen, who for whatever reasons, have slipped through the cracks. I am not saying everybody has to adopt my beliefs in regard to the Aboriginal community. What I'm saying is that those who oppose us do so in silence. The only man I can think of who triumphed over such prejudice is our Lord, Jesus Christ. He was not a cowardly man. He was not easily swayed by the opinions or gossip of his neighbours. Now, heaven knows, I am not my Lord, but I am a student of his love, and I try to be an honest teacher of his deeds, and I defy anyone here to pick up the bible and turn to the page where Jesus refuses any act of brotherhood to a person because of the colour of his skin!"

Of the thirty or so people left in the congregation, expressions ranged from open anxiety to contempt.

Still he could not think of a way to reach them. "It was recently brought to my attention that there are some in town who have given me the nickname 'Joe Coon.' Well, if that's what it takes. It makes no difference to my stand. This church will continue. The school that operates under its auspices will continue. Call me boneheaded. Hell, call me Irish. I am doing the Lord's work, and that is all that matters to me. But please, would you go home this morning and look at your own children, or grandchildren, or nieces and nephews and ask yourselves how you would feel if they were denied a decent education, a decent start in life? What would you do to make sure they had that start? I realise what I am asking you to do is difficult. Put the colour of their skin aside and see them as the children they are. If you can do that, for even a split second, you will see them as I do. These children I teach are not asking you for anything except a safe place to learn. I am asking that you at least question your views on race. My kids just want to show up tomorrow and learn. Now, so far as it is possible, let us keep an open mind and pray."

Before he had finished, two more couples and an angry-looking young woman stormed out. The church being only half full, the defections were noted keenly by the rest of the congregation.

Soon he was dejectedly sipping lukewarm coffee and trapped in another random conversation with Frank Dufford. This custom of fellowship with his congregation after the service had delighted the Father until now. He felt a part of the town, consoling a crying baby who had dropped her biscuit onto the dusty floor. Listening to a fishermen complain about the size of his catch that week. Sympathising as Mrs Clifford tried to show him the cataract in her eye, which was being operated on the following week (and boy wasn't she nervous). He was often reminded of his mother, Lydia, in groups like this. Even when his mother was emotionally burned out from living with a violent, belligerent drunk, she would tell him there wasn't a problem in the world that wasn't halved by sharing it with another. Father Joe Macaffery didn't learn his people skills at a seminary; he learned them from Lydia Macaffery, whom he remembered bursting into merriment at some Irish witticism and who always had an ear for some poor sod to pour his troubles into.

When he thought of what he had tried to do today, Father Joe believed absolutely that he had failed his kids. Certainly there were those here who thought their mere presence aligned them with God's purpose, just as long as they weren't asked to participate actively, which might grate with their long-held view of the world as they believed it should be.

He spotted Giselle manoeuvring over to the coffee urn with the flair of the long-time disabled, and found a flimsy excuse to extricate himself from Frank Dufford's clumsy conversation.

Giselle smiled at him warmly. "Father Macaffery, would you like another cup of coffee, sir?"

"Giselle, what I would like is a very dry martini, hold the vegetables."

"Oh dear, poor old Frank can't be that artless. He used to cut my grass, you know? I wanted to tell you that I loved your sermon. You stood up to them, Father. Good for you!"

"Not that it did my kids any good. I think perhaps all I did was rub salt into an open wound."

"Father Macaffery, if you were Jewish, I swear you wouldn't have one article of clothing that wasn't ripped to shreds. You have thrown down the gauntlet, good sir. Now you have to sit back with your students and see what, if any, difference it makes. You have something that our illustrious Grady Samuels does not have. You have time. You only have to sit back quietly and watch. Every day that goes by when he doesn't have anything to harp on about solidifies your position."

"You know there are only two women in my life I never interrupt, because you're both so bloody smart."

"Speaking of whom . . . if it's all right with you, I would like to meet her one day."

"Who?"

"Your Ma Bess."

"How do you know about Ma?"

Giselle grinned wickedly and patted the armrest of her chair. "When you're this close to the ground, you're apt to hear a great deal that passes most folk by. I hear she's something close to a deity out there, and that her tongue can curl the toes of a dead man. I've already decided I like the lady, Father. I like the lady a lot."

"I don't know. You two together could dethrone kings."

"It's a slightly lesser elected official I have in mind, Father. There is another matter I want to take up with you, while we're together. It's this 'I,' 'my,' position you have taken up regarding your students."

Father Joe looked at her in confusion.

"In your sermon, you kept saying 'my' kids," Giselle explained. "They are 'our' kids, Father, and they deserve to know they have more than one renegade priest in their corner, that's all I'm saying."

Any possible reply was cut off by a deep, throaty growl from the doorway. "Father Macaffery, could I speak to you for a minute?"

Father Joe saw all six-foot-four inches of Max Harris's brawny, bearded muscle, wading through the remainder of his congregation. When Father Joe had first arrived in Bindaree, he had heard the tale about the owner of the supermarket on Main Street. Once a member of an outlaw bikie gang, Max Harris had run foul of the law often, until the day he spotted five-foot-two Emily Follet, who had been on holiday from The Longvine College for Ladies, two doors down. Max had cut off his ponytail and dropped all underworld associations as quickly as he dropped his bandana. It took him two years to woo Emily, and another year for her to be sure the changes would stick, and then she married him. It was said to be one of the happiest marriages in Bindaree. Right now, Max looked red and flustered.

"Sorry. I was just wonderin' where you wanted the milk, and then Em and I will be off." He stood there expectantly.

Father Joe had not the slightest idea what he was talking about. "Sorry, Max. Milk, you said? I'm not sure I understand."

"Don't tell me you're giving those young 'uns Coca Cola, Father, 'cause that's no good for them."

"The kids drink water, Max. Like me. You said something about milk?"

"Well, it's Em, Father. She can't abide the idea of them kids learnin' on an empty stomach, so every Monday I'm gonna drop off a load of fresh milk and bread, if that's OK with you?"

Father Joe looked from Max to Giselle, whose face blushed red with pride, and sprayed laughter.

Max Harris just looked perplexed. "If you don't mind me sayin', you're behavin' kind of nutty, Father."

Father Joe clapped Max on the shoulder. "I'm sorry, Max. But we haven't had much to laugh about around here just lately, and then you come in with this incredible gesture. It's more than a sane man can take. I'd love you to drop off whatever pleases you for as long as it pleases you. Please leave it underneath the overhang in between the presbytery and the church. We're mighty grateful, Max. You tell that pretty wife of yours that her blood's worth bottling."

"Will do, Father. The overhang? I've got it. Take care now." Max blundered back the way he had come. Father Joe and Giselle looked at each other.

"You see, Father. It's 'our' kids, not 'mine'—not anymore."

CHAPTER 9

Father Joe sobered considerably two days later, when two policemen escorted a handcuffed Freddy Fingers through the doors of the church. The Father could immediately see how frightened the boy was. He stumbled down the aisle, towards the silent, staring class, like a groom about to marry the spectre of his darkest nightmare.

"Father Joe Macaffery?" asked the elder officer.

"That would be me, Officer. Can I ask what this is about?"

"Father, I . . ." began a hapless Freddy.

"Be quiet, Freddy. I was speaking to the officer?"

"Constable Egan," the policeman introduced himself. "This boy was discovered trying to stuff a bottle of Jim Beam down the front of his overalls in Max Harris's place. When approached by Mrs Harris, he threw the bottle at her and ran like the dickens. We caught up to him on Cutler Street."

In that moment, Father Joe was less concerned with Freddy's plight than he was angry with the boy. That it should be the Harris's, of all people, pained him, but he recognised that he had to handle the situation with tact. The words of his sermon came back to haunt him: "*We are not talking about juvenile delinquents or kids run foul of the law.*" All of a sudden, he felt very tired.

"If you would be so kind, could we take this conversation into the presbytery, where there is less of a captive audience? And may I request that you remove the handcuffs? He won't run."

Constable Egan considered that briefly and nodded. When they were inside his office, Father Joe requested he be allowed to phone Max Harris immediately. Constable Egan thought it strange he didn't call the boy's parents first, not knowing that Freddy didn't have the phone on at home. Max answered the phone after the first ring.

"Max, it's Father Macaffery, I just wanted to tell you how sorry I am for what happened this morning. I will make this up to you. I promise."

"It's OK, Father. He put the fear of the devil into Em, smashing that bottle at her like that, but she's not hurt and we won't be pressing charges."

"Could you tell Emily how sorry I am, please? And would it be all right with both of you if I brought the boy over at ten tomorrow morning to apologise?"

"That'd be fine, Father. Then I'd just as soon the matter was finished."

"I understand, Max. You have my word."

Father Joe put the phone down and turned to the officers and the white-faced boy.

"Father, I'm really sorry, I—" he began again.

Father Joe looked at the stern, tired-looking Constable Egan. "I said be quiet, Freddy. Constable Egan, the cuffs, if you don't mind."

Constable Derek Egan had heard about the priest's school. He thought the situation a strange one, but it was two-thirty and he had been on duty since six in the morning. More than anything, he wanted this shift to end so he could collapse into the arms of his wife for the night and not worry about thieving blacks and their strange, priestly benefactor. He removed the cuffs from Freddy, wrenching the boy's shoulder up a little higher than was necessary, just to remind the kid that there was always a next time.

"I think you should know that he refused to give us his surname."

"Freddy, tell the officers your name."

"Freddy Fingers, Father."

"My patience is wearing very thin. Your last name—now boy!"

The boy stared at him miserably. "Frederick James Nagawalli," he whispered.

"There you have it. Mr and Mrs Harris aren't pressing charges, and I will personally vouch that nothing like this will ever happen again. If there is nothing else, you can leave the boy here with me."

Officer Egan just nodded wearily. He was relieved. What happened now was on the priest's head, not his.

"I'll follow you out, if I may," said Father Joe. "I have to explain this to my class." He looked at Freddy. "Lad, don't you shift your butt from that chair until I tell you otherwise or you won't be able to sit down for a week."

As the police were leaving the church, Father Joe asked, "May I ask, who told you to bring the boy to me?"

"You have friends in high places, Father. It was Mayor Samuels."

Father Joe winced. He didn't want to think about the potential fallout from this. It was just the sort of thing Grady Samuels would salivate over.

As soon as the police left, the class erupted in argument over what they should do with Freddy. Father Joe, knowing many Aborigines almost pathologically mistrusted the police, was surprised the kids were so disgusted with Freddy and were concerned about the shame they felt he had brought upon them. It was an insight into how they felt about their school. For the first time since Career's Day, Doyle and Gunther were of the same opinion.

Doyle, still aching over his break up with Lilly, pronounced Freddy a liability. "He's no good, Father. We'd best be done with him. He hasn't been doing any of the work we've been doing anyway."

It surprised Father Joe when Gunther chimed in. "When coppers start coming in here, we've got trouble, Father. It's just the ammo some folks need to try breaking us up. You can reach a lot of kids, Father, but even you told me there will always be ones that you can't." Gunther didn't look at Father Joe, but addressed the whole class with confidence.

"OK, I have to go back in there and deal with Freddy now. Gunther, would you like to call Ma Bess and ask her to pick you lot up early today? The rest of you, I will take what you said into consideration. See you tomorrow."

Gunther followed him through into the office to call Ma. Freddy had been crying but hadn't moved a muscle. No doubt he had heard some of the conversation outside and was worried about his fate. Father Joe found him a clean hanky and waited until Gunther had used the phone before he said, "You surprised me just now, Gunther. I didn't think you would discard a friend quite so casually. You usually have more compassion than that."

Gunther blushed but met the Father's eyes. Then he turned to Freddy. "I think of you as a mate, but you haven't been taking this seriously. You're still doing the same stupid stuff we were doing before we had this school. I don't know what you'd like to do one day, but I know you won't be doing anything if you goof off all the time. I don't know if you're capable of changing, Freddy. I hope so, but I just don't know." Gunther's brown eyes returned to Father Joe. "I'm sorry to have disappointed you, Father. I'll see you tomorrow."

Freddy burst into a fresh torrent of tears as Gunther left them. He still looked scared. "What are you going to do to me, Father?"

"Well, boy, you screwed up big time, but there isn't a lot I can do. I am going to take you down to the Harris's tomorrow at ten, and you are going to apologise to Mr and Mrs Harris."

"What if I'm not here tomorrow?" asked the boy slyly, through his tears.

"Then I'll go myself and apologise to two people who have become great friends of this school. I can't force you to come to school, Freddy. I can't set you on the straight and narrow and make sure you stay on it. That's not the way I work. Most of the kids who come here want to be here. Disruptions like this screw them up too, and since you call some of them your friends, I should think you wouldn't want them to think of you as nothing but a lazy thief. You have to make a decision. I can't help you with it this time."

Freddy stopped crying. When he looked at Father Joe, he saw only kindness reflected back at him.

"But I've missed a lot of work. I don't know if I can catch up."

"Well, isn't it lucky for you that I know of one slightly beat-up Irishman who will make it his mission in life to help you catch up. It's not too late, Freddy."

"If I come tomorrow, do you have to take me back there to apologise?"

"Yes, I do. There are some things in life you can't run away from. Your actions today hurt people, and you have to deal with that. A good man takes responsibility for his actions."

The boy still looked lost. "Can I go now, Father?"

Father Joe wanted to help him, wanted to understand him. He just didn't know if Freddy would give him the chance. "Yes, Freddy Fingers, you can go now. Just remember one thing for me: anybody can make a mistake, it takes a man to own up to it."

Freddy left quickly and quietly, leaving Father Joe with no clue if he would see him tomorrow.

★ ★ ★

Two hours later a large, agitated-looking woman with three blackened teeth waddled into the presbytery and identified herself as Myrtle Nagawilli, Freddy's mother. Myrtle gave off the powerful combined aromas of marijuana and Cashmere Bouquet talcum powder. And Lord, could she talk. She was one of the most garrulous people Father Joe had ever met.

He soon learned he had only nanoseconds in which to cram in any questions, otherwise Myrtle would just bulldoze right over the top of him with barely a pause for breath. On the subject of Freddy's intellect, she had a circus carney's soapbox ready to climb upon.

"He's dim-witted, Father, and it ain't nobody's fault, that's just the way he came out!"

"Mrs Nagawilli—"

"Oh, call me Myrtle, Father, because 'Mrs Nagawilli' makes me look around for my mother, and believe me when I tell you life's a lot sweeter since that old bitch carked it!"

Father Joe couldn't help but smile, perhaps in gratitude that he didn't have talk to the, lovingly referred to, deceased as well, who had no doubt been as loquacious as her daughter.

"Myrtle, I think with some extra help, if he puts his head down, Freddy could do really well, and I'm willing to spend my Friday mornings tutoring him."

Myrtle looked at him as if he had recently lost his mind. "That's a wonderful gesture, Father, but, believe me, it would be a waste of your time. Freddy's older brother Raymond was the smart one in the family. He was always reading. He'd read everything, Father, and if he didn't know a word, well then he'd go and look it up. I always thought Raymond would grow up to be one of those scholarly types and that young Freddy would make a good gardener or custodian, or he might eventually get a labouring job of some sort, I suppose, but I'm sorry to say you got the wrong brother, Father."

"If you don't mind my asking, Myrtle, what happened to Raymond?"

"Ah, the needle took him, I found them when I came home one afternoon—when I used to work, that is, you know I can't now on account of my varicose veins—Freddy was screaming for me and Raymond was stone, cold dead, still had the needle in his arm. They said the heroin was laced with something, but

I disremember what and it was eight years ago now, Father, and Ray would be twenty-five next month. It's plain wrong, Father, Raymond being so smart and all and God took him from me and left me Freddy who is the mental equivalent of a Whoopi cushion and I'll have him for years yet."

"You said that Freddy called out to you. It was Freddy who found Raymond?"

"Yeah, a regular Johnny-on-the-spot, that boy and I know what you're thinking, but it didn't seem to bother him overmuch—oh sure, he had a couple of quiet days after it, but then the whole family was grieving and you of all people should know what that's like, Father, so I'm just warning you that Freddy ain't goin' to be no Einstein, no matter what you do, but beggin' your pardon, if you want to fight some fool's crusade with my youngest, I'll not stand in your way."

"Thank you, Myrtle. Put it this way, at least he'll be out from under your feet and not getting into anymore mischief."

"Right you are, Father, but just you remember I done warned you beforehand."

He watched Myrtle Nagawilli as she wheezed and stomped off toward Cutler Street, her shoes covered in the red dust of The Res, her caftan wet with large sweat stains under her arms. At least, after unravelling some of the strings of young Freddy's less than idyllic childhood, he knew what he was up against.

★   ★   ★

"Myrtle Nagawilli is a fool, and only a fool would pay attention to anything she says," said Ma Bess.

"I had to hear her out, Ma. She's the boy's mother."

"Yes, and for that, young Freddy has my sincere condolences."

They were sitting in the dining area of Ma's van, Father Joe with a coffee and Ma Bess nursing a beer.

"Did you know her when she lost Raymond, the oldest son?"

Ma threw him a disgusted expression. "Course I did. Old enough to be Methuselah, ain't I? I know everyone! Myrtle thought the sun shone out of Raymond's arse. Hell, he might have had a brain too, but how would you know? He was loaded all the time. Old Myrtle put all her eggs in one basket and then heroin squashed it flat. I've seen it before with dogs. The bitch favours one of the pups so much that the others just sort of hang on her, forgotten about, gettin' smaller and smaller. If they survive at all it's a miracle."

"All I know is that the lad needs help."

"Don't tell me you just happen to have nothing to do on Friday mornings, Joe. Whitey is already plenty pissed about who you're keeping company with." She leaned over and grabbed the collar of his shirt. "Take that thing off and give it to me."

Father Joe grabbed the collar of his shirt warily as Ma got up and began rummaging in one of the kitchen drawers.

"Why am I taking my shirt off, Ma?"

"So, I can mend it, you idiot. You've got three buttons about ready to fall off. Men never look after themselves proper. C'mon, strip!"

"Are you sure?"

Pulling out her sewing kit, she grinned wickedly at him. "Why, Joe, did you think you were about to get lucky? I hate to douse your flames, big boy, but you're not my type. Too bloody pale!"

Blushing Irish red, Father Joe removed his shirt and handed it to her.

"Of course," she said cheekily, 'If Percy happens on by, he'll insist on duelling you for my honour."

She had supplied the opening for a question he had been burning to ask. "About Percy, Ma. I know you two are close . . ."

Ma raised an eyebrow and smiled cheekily at him.

"I was just wondering if I might have done something to upset him. He doesn't seem to like me very much."

Ma was still staring at him, over her reading glasses, but her expression sobered. "And you're not used to anyone not liking you, are you, Joe? Affable son-of-a-bitch, that you are!"

"Not when I don't know the reason for it, no."

Ma continued mending his neglected shirt, obviously thinking. Finally she said, "OK, I'm going to tell it to you straight. Percy doesn't like you. First, because you're a white man. And second, because you're a priest. You see, when Percy was eight years old, he was separated from his mother and sent to live in a Christian boy's home. Said it was a real hellhole. The priests there abused him, he told me. The first year he was there, he cried every day. When he aged out, he went lookin' for his mother, but she had died of a heart attack, scrubbing some white woman's floor long before he got out. As was the case in those days, if you were an Abo, your grave wasn't marked. Percy saved money out of his first few paychecks to buy her a headstone. So, he'd know where his mother rested. So, you see Joe, to Percy, you went and bit the apple twice: a white man and a priest. I'm sorry, but you've got the weight of history workin' against you." She peered over the top of her glasses again and shrugged. "Those stolen generations the politicians prattle on about? Well, Percy is one of the stolen. The life that man has led has taken a toll on him all right, but he's always been a decent enough bloke to me."

Father Joe's stomach flipped as if he had eaten something greasy. He bore enough guilt over his own sins; he didn't need to take on any more, and certainly not over something he had no ownership in. Yet it was consternation he felt. Percy's barely concealed resentment bothered him because, just as he had told John Kutukutu, he wasn't used to being judged for the sins of others. "I don't suppose you could put in a good word for me, Ma? I think he'd listen to you."

Ma snorted scornfully. "You bet your lily-white arse, he would. Percy knows I've got a stake in the school, and he'll stay out of my way because he's not an ignorant black, no matter what some people think. As for putting in a good word for you, I've already done that. We've struck a compromise. You and I have business doin's together and Percy's promised to stay out of them and not to mouth off to you. If the old bastard craves my company so much, than he'll behave himself and keep a civil tongue in his head."

"Civil tongue, Ma? The man is practically mute in my presence. Maybe, I should talk to him?"

Ma took off her glasses and stared at him—hard. "Joe, I didn't get to this age by being stupid or cowardly. Sometimes, you gotta know when to stand aside and let fate iron out any wrinkles in your life. I'm trying to be kind, because I like you, but the best thing for you to do is to stay out of old Percy's business and he'll stay out of yours, OK?"

He sighed and gave her a lame smile. "OK, Ma. You know best."

"Joe, I shouldn't have to keep telling you that happy fact. You white fellas don't learn very quickly, do you?" She threw the mended shirt at him. "Now, put that back on and clear out, I've got work to attend to and you're chewing up my day."

*   *   *

The next morning, before the sun had nudged over the horizon, Father Joe was woken by the smell of freshly brewing coffee and the sound of someone moving furtively around his kitchen while still managing to make a racket only the devil could beat. His alarm clock said it was not even half past four, but the aroma of coffee was finally too much for him. Of course, he knew who his early morning visitor was.

"If that's a burglar in my kitchen, take what you want, just leave the coffee. If it's Gunther Pearce, may I ask what in hell you are doing here this early?"

"Morning, Father," yelled the boy. "Sorry, I didn't mean to be so noisy. I've got coffee and the paper."

Father Joe stumbled into the kitchen and looked at the boy. "Gunther, my boy, you know I love you, but there must be something mighty that's preying on your mind for you to be here at this hour. Spit it out."

Gunther looked embarrassed, but finally blurted out what was choking him. "It's about Freddy, Father. What you said yesterday, about me not having enough compassion, is that what you really think? Perhaps I did come down on Freddy too harshly. I was just trying to think about the best interests of the school. I thought I explained myself pretty clearly, but perhaps I should have kept my opinion to myself."

Father Joe wondered how long Gunther had lain awake last night, replaying the conversation in his mind. He knew the boy regarded him highly, and if he was honest with himself, the criticism he had levelled at Gunther yesterday was born out of his own feelings of inadequacy. He remembered something Father Gus had told him a long time ago. That when you love someone, you take responsibility for them. The last thing he wanted to do was to hurt the lad.

"Gunther, you had an opinion and you expressed it. When I made that stupid comment, I hadn't any more time than you to process the situation. You told Freddy how you felt. You can't be a better friend than that. I don't know if Freddy will change his ways or not, but what you said was honest. Upon reflection, it was probably just what Freddy needed to hear. So, don't lose any more sleep. More importantly, don't lose any more of my sleep. Do your folks even know where you are?"

"Sure. Every morning I write them a note telling them what I'm doing that day. This morning I told them I needed to make you some strong coffee, so you can go out and surf before trying to teach our lazy bones something. They cope just fine."

"As long as they're OK, I suppose. Now, did you brew that coffee just to tease me or are you going to pour me a cup?"

The boy laughed, and it seemed that a weight had been lifted off him. His eyes, beneath incredibly long lashes, sparkled as he poured Father Joe a cup of coffee. The Father was left wondering how a spirit as pure as Gunther's had attached its star to his rusty little red wagon.

Later that morning, when the Ma Bess Express pulled in beside the church, Father Joe was heartened to see the lady herself exit the van accompanied by Freddy, who was groomed to within an inch of his life and carrying a small bouquet of

carnations wrapped in aluminium foil. Ma Bess clamped a hand
on the boy's shoulder and, as usual, didn't mess around. "Hey
Joe, I've got an early birthday present for you. I've brought you
one very repentant sinner. I hear you two have a little business to
take care of this morning."

"Thanks, Ma." Father Joe then turned to the boy. Freddy
looked very clean. He also looked very pale, for an Aboriginal
boy. "Hello, Freddy. You hardly look like the same boy who left
here yesterday. I'm glad you decided to join us. I promise I'll
help you catch up with the rest of the class. You just concentrate
on doing the best you can."

Father Joe realised the idea of confronting the Harris's was
more frightening than being caught by the cops. Boys from The
Res weren't often put in the situation of having to atone for their
misdeeds. More often than not, they got away with things or got
a whipping as punishment, with no thought to compensate their
victims.

"I got these flowers to give to Mrs Harris, Father. I don't
know if she'll want them, but Ma said it was a nice thing to do.
You'll be with me, Father?"

"I will, and you'll be fine, lad. If it helps, doing a thing is
nearly always easier than thinking about it. Now, go on inside
while I talk to Ma for a bit."

The boy cut a forlorn figure, walking into church in his
Sunday best. Father Joe hurt for him.

"Joe, you've got a problem, my man," said Ma.

"And I'm sure you're just the wise woman to tell me what
that problem is?"

Ma scowled. "You're getting too attached to these kiddies.
Don't get me wrong, how you've treated young Freddy's situation is
wonderful, but I'm afraid you're investing more than you can afford

to lose. What if tomorrow Freddy up and decides to hell with
schooling, I'll go into business with Victor Dumagee instead?"

"I'll cross that bridge if I come to it. You're a regular
doomsayer today, Ma. You can't tell me you don't see the change
in those kids."

"I can. And part of me loves what I'm seeing. But just
remember, at the end of the day, most of them are going home
to The Res. They'll be lucky if they can survive their childhood
in one piece. I'm just saying, maybe it's time to pull back a little,
get a little objectivity. If you don't, I'm predicting you're going
to get your heart stomped."

Once again, Father Joe found himself touched by her
concern. "Ma, I don't think you understand. I came from a
home where the only thing you needed was a reputation and a
right hook. And I made a reputation for myself all right. I was a
nasty bastard, with no respect for anyone or anything. I thought
religion was for pussies. One night, I did something I can never
take back. But with the help of a very patient friend, I decided
I really wanted to get out of the environment I was in, and I
wanted to help people. So I came here, to Bindaree, to try to
start a new life, try to pay it forward."

Ma Bess's expression softened. "What about whitey, Joe. Do
you really think they're going to sit back and take this much
longer? You can cut the atmosphere in this town with a knife.
You've gone and made it a question of pride now. How do you
propose to deal with them?"

"I won't have to deal with anyone, Ma. I have to believe
the boss has his eye on me." Father Joe nodded skyward. "He's
ready to redirect me if I wander off course. It's my job to do the
best by these kids that I can. I really believe that's what he wants
from me."

Ma shook her head slowly. "I've got a feeling your lily-white arse is going to get hurt, Joe. I feel it in my bones. I'm no Jesus Jumper, as you well know, but I'll say a little prayer for you all the same. Just don't expect me to start coming to your bloody church, you hear? I can't stand that 'you've won a lottery ticket to heaven' crap."

"Wouldn't dream of it, Ma. If I'm a little cocky, it's because, with you and the good Lord on my side, how can I lose?"

Ma's face clouded over with a stern expression that Father Joe thought of as her 'don't fuck with me' face.

"Be glib if you want," she said. "I'm just going to tell you this one time. When you're black, you get used to losing. Hell, it's damn near a lifelong occupation, and as you like to point out, being Irish is damn near the same thing. I don't want to see you lose, Joe."

She left shortly afterwards, but her concern remained a blemish on his mind for the rest of the day. It was the closest she would ever come to saying I love you, or I believe in you.

Father Joe supposed he was guilty of being too proud of the school's accomplishments, but he wanted her to share in them with him. The old adage was right, it did take a village to raise a child, and Ma was an integral part of that village. That she was so worried about him and the kids bothered him a lot more than he cared to admit.

At nine-forty-five a.m., Father Joe left Gunther in charge of the class, and he and Freddy left to see Max and Emily Harris. On the ride there the boy was sitting ramrod straight, a Parkinson-like tremor running through his body. Whatever brash idiocy had overtaken him the day before had clearly forsaken him this morning. Father Joe's heart went out to him, but he knew that this admission of guilt was central to the boy's long-term growth. Twice, Freddy had asked nervously if the Father would come into the shop with him while he apologised. Father Joe had twice assured him that he would. When they arrived, Max Harris was behind the till. He fixed Freddy with a baleful glare that would have made most adults quake in their boots, and then he went into the back of the shop to find Emily. The couple came out together to meet them.

Father Joe introduced them to Freddy, whose voice barely rose above a whisper as he said, "Mr and Mrs Harris, I want to say that I'm really sorry for what I did yesterday. What I did was wrong, and I promise I'll never try to steal anything again." Realising that he still clutched the bunch of carnations, he thrust them at Emily Harris.

Accepting the meagre bouquet, Emily said, "You did give me a scare, young man, but I hope you've learned your lesson. You shouldn't be drinking at your age anyway. Your brain hasn't finished growing yet. Alcohol will only damage it. Why weren't you in school in the middle of the day?"

Freddy looked embarrassed. "I fell behind the others. I'm not as smart as they are."

Emily looked on him with genuine pity. "Well, no matter how frightened and angry you made me yesterday, I don't think you're a bad boy, Freddy."

A glimpse of a smile appeared on Freddy's face. "Thank you, Ma'am."

Max turned to Father Joe. "This won't change our arrangement with the groceries, Father. The boy and his friends need taking care of, and Em and I still intend to do our part."

"Thank you both. You're very generous and very forgiving. I'll be sure to include you both in my prayers. However, right now, I'd better get this lad back to school so he can hit the books."

Both sides parted amicably, and Father Joe noticed Freddy had lost the tremor that had plagued him a half-hour before.

"Father, they were really nice to me. I was expecting they'd hate me. Jesus, that Mr Harris is a big dude, isn't he? I'm not going to steal anything ever again, Father."

Father Joe reached over and ruffled the boy's hair. "That's good to know, lad. Eventually, you'll learn that the things you work for mean more than anything you can steal. Besides, you're better than that, Freddy. I know it, and you should to."

Freddy didn't reply, but he had a smile on his face. When he entered the church, there was no sign of the animosity that had enveloped the class the day before. They welcomed Freddy back as if he had been away sick for a few days.

After class, Father Joe called him over. "OK, Freddy, you're in school again. We work four days a week, instead of The Potter School's five, simply because we cram five days' work into four. Because you are behind in a few subjects, I'm going to propose that you come in on Friday mornings. Together, you and I will soon have you caught up with the rest of the class. How does that sound to you?"

Freddy made a face like he had bitten into a fresh lemon. It was clear he wasn't excited by the prospect. "Isn't there another way, Father? So I don't have to come in on Fridays?"

"If there is an easier way, I don't know it. You want the results; you have to put in the work. It's that simple. I'll remind you that you're not the only person giving up their time and energy. I'm going to be spending time with you instead of with the few parishioners I have left."

The boy nodded slowly at that. "OK, Father, I'll do it. Just remember, I'm not as smart as the others."

"You'll be fine. It shouldn't take too long. Now, you had better scoot or you might brook the fury of Ma Bess, something no man wants, believe me."

Freddy Fingers kept his word. For the next five Fridays, he and Father Joe sat in the presbytery, listening to Father Joe's Elvis collection and cramming in as much information as Freddy was able to absorb. Father Joe continually praised and encouraged him. Freddy's inferiority complex had been carefully nurtured by Myrtle, who obviously didn't comprehend the millstone she had tied around the boy's neck. Years of being told he wasn't a patch on his dead brother—of not being good enough—had taken root. The one person who should have been bolstering his confidence all those years, had been systematically destroying it. Regardless, tutored by Father Joe, Freddy soon started to blossom. He caught up with the others, and Father Joe watched Freddy's former timidity in class vanish as the boy gained confidence. Freddy also read more and socialised better with the other kids. The energy Father Joe had put into Freddy's transformation seemed justified when he learned that Freddy was washing Max Harris's Jeep every week as a way of making up for the bungled robbery.

After a while, if Max Harris happened to be driving past during school hours, he would stop off to see how the boy was doing. He told Freddy about his life before Emily and how he could easily have been in jail right now himself. Ham-fisted Max made an unlikely Pygmalion, but it soon became evident that Freddy worshipped the man. Father Joe was careful not to make too big a deal of it, lest he embarrass the boy, but he inwardly cheered Freddy's progress.

CHAPTER 10

Unfortunately, not all the kids were happy in their present circumstances. Doyle's misery radiated outward, like an invisible mist that affected everyone around him. Lilly had not succumbed to his frantic attempts to win her back. He had not helped his cause in the month since Career's Day. His behaviour had been erratic, charming her one moment and cruelly ignoring her the next. He finally seemed satisfied that the only relationship between Lilly and Gunther was one of friendship, but he was jealous of it even so. Father Joe had tried talking to the boy, but what could he possibly say that would mend Doyle's first heartbreak?

Doyle's schoolwork reflected his current state. Where once he had read and studied because he wanted Lilly to be proud of him—to show her he intended to escape The Res and get away from his drunken father—now he couldn't seem to muster the energy to even participate in class.

The boy was heartsick, and Father Joe didn't know what to do about it. To the rest of the class, he was still top dog, and none of them knew a way to reach him either. Father Joe thought the real pity was that Lilly was clearly still crazy about Doyle. He could see how much it hurt her when Doyle deliberately ignored her. But Father Joe admired Lilly's determination to refuse to accept what she considered to be unacceptable behaviour.

Doyle's behaviour, in comparison, was juvenile and self-indulgent, and was inflamed by Tommy King's defection as his faithful sidekick. Tommy was still there in body, but his spirit was now focussed like a laser on his eligibility for the army.

"They're not going to let you in, mate." Father Joe overhead Doyle telling his friend afternoon at lunch.

"You're a bloody half-cast! Hell, they'll give a fag a gun before they'll give you one!"

"The Father rang ADFA," Tommy argued. "I have to complete the same requirements as everybody else."

Doyle shook his friend's ear, as if he were talking to a simpleton rather than to his best friend.

"You're not hearing me, Tommy. They say one thing to you sure, because they have to, but mark my words they'll find a way to keep you out. It'll never happen and you'll have wasted all this time for nothing. You have to face facts, you're black, mate, and there isn't anything in this country that's worse. I just don't want you to get hurt."

Father Joe interrupted by clamping a hand down on Doyle's shoulder. "Could I speak to you for a minute, lad?"

"Sure."

Father Joe waited until they were out of earshot before he spoke. "Lad, if I ever hear you talking like that to one of my students again, I will pack you off to The Res immediately and you won't be coming back, do you understand?"

"I'm his mate. I was just telling him the truth. You just treat him like a mushroom—keep him in the dark and feed him shit!"

"You've got a funny bloody view of mateship. A mate builds a person up; he doesn't tear him down. Just because you're not happy with your lot at the moment does not mean you take it out on others. Boy, I've given you some latitude, because I know you're working through some stuff, but if you ever speak to me like that again, you'll be running back to The Res. You know most of the kids look up to you, and you go off and spout that garbage. It's not happening on my watch. Am I clear?"

The boy scowled at him. "Crystal."

"Good. Now, lunch is over, get in there and do some work."

When Father Joe went to bed that night, Doyle's words to Tommy resounded in his head. *You're black, mate, and there isn't anything in this country that's worse.* How many of the kids felt as Doyle did? He didn't know, but by morning he had a plan to bust a hole right through that belief and eliminate the belief the kids harboured: that being black was the ultimate hardship and that those who weren't black couldn't understand the daily adversity they faced. It was a self-pitying attitude that Father Joe knew would only hold them back in life. But to defeat it, he needed to enlist specialised help. Giselle's help.

He asked Giselle in a halting uncertain way, very unlike his usual assured manner. He was unsure whether his request would cause her pain. She was an old lady, and with all she had been through, she deserved some peace in her last years. As usual, she surprised him.

"Of course, I'll do it, Father."

"Thank you so much. You're a very special lady."

She smiled up at him. "Don't you worry about me, Father Macaffery. I come from very hearty stock, and this way I get to meet your students, which I would just love. Also, you might invite the notorious Ma Bess. I would love to meet the woman who keeps you in line," she said cheekily.

"I'll put her top of the guest list."

"Splendid. Now that's sorted, what do you say to a little game of chess?"

★   ★   ★

By one o'clock the next Thursday, the class was getting fidgety. They knew something was up. Ma Bess had arrived early and was now sitting in a pew at the rear of the church, along with Percy and Jeremy Pindari. Father Joe had told them they were having a special guest and had gone to pick her up, leaving a raucous Mudguard in charge of the class. They were supposed to be tackling the long-division problems on the board, but two hours before the weekend started, the students displayed little interest in them.

When he heard the beep of Father Joe's horn, Gunther raced outside to help get Giselle's wheelchair out and push her inside. Long division was, mercifully, forgotten. Gunther wheeled Giselle into the centre of the church and Father Joe put a glass of water down next to his friend. He faced the kids and clapped his hands.

The room went quiet.

"Troops, I have a very important friend I want to introduce. She's going to talk to you for a few minutes as a personal favour to me, so you will be quiet, you will be respectful, and if you have a question you will wait until Ms Dresner has finished, put up your hand, introduce yourself and ask your question. Is that clear?"

A few kids nodded and let out Thursday-afternoon sighs.

"I said, is that clear?" Father Joe hollered at them.

This time, he got a full complement of "Yes, Fathers," except for Doyle, who rested his head on his desk, silent and disinterested.

"Thank you. This is my friend Giselle Dresner."

Giselle looked smaller and older sitting in front of the pulpit, where the infamous red brick rested. She looked at the shiny, bright-eyed faces with something close to wonder. Father Macaffery had asked a favour of her, and she would try to come through for him and these children, who were at the beginning of their journey, even as she sat there towards the end of hers. All she could do was tell them the truth.

"My name is Giselle Dresner and I am eighty-three years old. And I am Jewish. I have lived in Australia for many years now and I think it's the best country in the world, but when I was young, about the same age as some of you, I lived in a city called Lodz, in Poland. Father Macaffery tells me you are studying World War Two. Well, I was there in the middle of it. During the war, the Nazis swept through Europe with one singular goal—to kill every Jew in Europe."

Giselle spoke calmly of the horrors she had lived through. Many she had never divulged in detail before, not even to Eve.

"Adolf Hitler was a madman. First, Jews were not allowed in shops or in schools. We were not allowed to worship. We were not allowed to drink from public fountains or use public pools. We were thrown out of our homes and made to live in ghettos. In the ghettos, there were no jobs, no food or sanitation. We would regularly walk past dead bodies on the street. We were made to wear a Star of David at all times so that good Germans could distinguish between them and us.

"Hitler gave one of his lackeys, a man named Adolf Eichmann, the task of getting rid of us Jews. Eichmann's first plan was to send all the Jews in Europe to the island of Madagascar. When that proved unrealistic, he came up with a proposition he called, "The Final Solution to The Jewish Question." Its purpose was to exterminate all Jews. To kill all of us!" Giselle's disguised a hitch in her throat by sipping at the glass of water. She had every child's attention now, even Doyle's, although it was hard to read what he was thinking.

She continued, "The Germans built concentration camps where they could begin what they called the 'orderly disposal' of Jews. They gassed us with something called Zyklon B, which killed us. They had other prisoners collect the bodies and take them to the ovens to be cremated. I remember the sky used to be a constant plume of smoke, so thick it would cover everything, including those of us who were kept alive to work. You see, the Nazis believed in doing things efficiently, so when you were transported to a camp, they would give you a number and tattoo it on your wrist. From that moment on, you were not considered a person anymore, you were just a number, and you waited to die.

"In your studies you may have already heard the name Auschwitz. Over a million people were killed there. That is where my mother, my grandmother and I were imprisoned. The irony is that my mother survived that hellhole, but she died during liberation—of typhus. We were told my father and grandfather went to Belsen and were shot the day after they arrived, but we could never be sure. People died every day in

Auschwitz. Towards the end of the war, the Nazis went into a killing frenzy.

"Disease was rampant. People dropped dead where they were standing."

The church was silent. As Father Joe listened to his friend speak, he watched the faces of the kids. They were captivated by her story, completely focused as she described the barracks and daily life at Auschwitz. Other than Giselle's gentle voice, the only other sounds for the next half-an-hour were the creak of someone's chair as they shifted position and the wind whistling through the boarded-up, broken window.

Giselle looked around the church as she spoke, watching Father Macaffery and the worried expression on his face.

"Where was I? Yes, people died where they stood, mostly from disease and starvation. Rudolf Höss was the commandant of the camp. In history he would be known as 'The Death Dealer of Auschwitz.' He used to set his dogs on prisoners. They would literally rip the throat out of a person. He did this for fun, you understand?" She was crying quietly now.

Father Macaffery went up to her with a hanky. "Giselle, we can leave it there for today. I'm sorry I asked you to do this."

Giselle gripped the armrests of her chair. She wasn't budging until she had said what she came to say. She smiled at the faces in the church and said, "No, Father. I think I need to tell this as much as your kids need to hear it. I'm ready to continue now." Turning back to face the kids, she said, "I'm sorry for getting emotional. But, you see, I've never actually talked about this before. Not even to my closest friends." The kids were silent, trying with their unsophisticated minds to fully grasp the horror of her story. "Over and over again, we Jewish prisoners were told we weren't human beings. We were rats, like the vermin we were forced to live with; and the same as the rats, we had to be exterminated for the good of the new Nazi-inherited Europe.

"All the time we wore the yellow Star of David to proclaim our Jewishness and the numbers on our wrists became more familiar to us than our own names. My number was 11,379, and it is still inked on my wrist. It doesn't anger me as much as it used to do. When I look at it now, I think of it as my survivor's number.

"Nazi Germany was not the only time Jewish people were persecuted. We may be white, but believe me, we have been hated through the ages, and not always for reasons I understand. Just as I don't understand why I survived and so many others didn't. Perhaps, Father Macaffery's God knows the answer, but I am just an old woman who wears the Star of David now to say, 'Yes, world, I am a Jew and I survived, and of course, to honour those who didn't." Giselle folded her hands together in her lap. "I want to say a big thank you to all of them. Someone once said it was important to remember the events of the past, so that they could be understood and the mistakes never repeated. Well, the only caveat to that theory is Auschwitz. You could rack you brains for years and I doubt you could understand such evil. I can't, and I was there.

"Anyway, Father Macaffery has told me some of your troubles and I just wanted to let you know that they may seem big now, but they are not so bad that you can't overcome them. You are young. You have friends, and no matter some people's prejudices, in this country at least, you are seen as human beings, not numbers. I hope what I've told you today helps you to understand that you don't have to be black to be the subject of hatred. And even if you are, you can fight against it. That's the thing to do—to fight racism wherever you find it. That's all I really wanted to say. Thank you."

She stopped talking. Silence, taut as a rope, filled the church. The kids looked shell-shocked, trying to process what they had just heard. Then, of their own accord, led by a surprisingly earnest-looking Mudguard, they stood up and clapped.

"Does anyone have anything they would like to ask me?" asked Giselle.

Once again, Mudguard's errant hand was the first one up. "Excuse me, Ms Dresner, my name is Mudguard. I was wondering if I could see your tattoo?"

"Mudguard!" thundered Father Joe.

"No, it's fine, Father. He can see it."

Gracious as ever, Giselle held out her wrist so that Mudguard and the other openly curious kids could see the inked number.

"You have a very unique name, Mudguard."

Studying her wrist intently, the boy said, "It's faint."

"It's very old now."

Tommy raised his hand next. "I'm Tommy King, Ms Dresner. How long were you in Auschwitz?"

"Two and a half years, Tommy. I had my fourteenth birthday there."

Gunther raised his hand. "My name is Gunther, Ms Dresner. Thanks for coming and talking to us this afternoon. Why did everyone think so badly of the Jews? I mean, why did they think you were dishonest and stuff?"

"Hello, Gunther. I've seen you in church. To answer your question, Adolf Hitler ensured he had men around him, Eichmann and many more, who were just as corrupt as he was. He employed a man named Joseph Goebbels to be his Minister for Propaganda. It was his job to lie about and disparage the

Jews. Goebbels once famously said about lying: 'If you tell a lie big enough and keep repeating it, people will eventually come to believe it.' Hitler, Eichmann and Goebbels were all bullies. Only they didn't steal your lunch money or push you over in the playground, they controlled an army that was powerful and deadly."

"Why didn't you just leave and go somewhere else, where there were no Nazis?" asked Gunther.

"Because I was born in Poland. It was my home. Our home had been in the Dresner family for eighty years. I know people who went to make a home in Israel. But my mother raised me not to run away from anyone who is trying to wallop the tar out of me. Maybe if I had known what would happen in Europe, but it's too late to speculate on that now. I want you to know that you've got a powerful and loyal friend here in the Father. I hope you all appreciate that."

The kids looked a little self-conscious, but they allowed that, yes, Father Joe was their guy. After the questions had dried up and Freddy had gone to get another glass of water for Giselle, Father Joe excused the kids, telling them to wait outside for Ma Bess, who would be out shortly. Father Joe wanted to make sure that what Giselle had done for them wasn't more than she could bear.

"Honestly, I'm fine, Father. I admit I've never really told anyone that much before, but it might have been for the good. I just hope I didn't say anything inappropriate."

Father Joe's smile was rueful. "There's not much that is appropriate about the Holocaust. No, I hope the kids had a bit of an awakening today. Under the circumstances, I can't see that's a bad thing."

He didn't realise Ma Bess was still there until she came up behind him and clapped him hard on the shoulder. "Have you forgotten your manners, Preacher?"

"No, Ma'am. Giselle, this is the formidable Ma Bess, and her good friend Percy."

Ma scoffed at him and turned to Giselle. "Have you ever met a man more full of shit than this one? You know he's told me a bit about you. Thank you for coming and talking to the kiddies. It was good of you."

"He never shuts up about you Ma, and talking to the kids was my pleasure. They're a polite, inquisitive lot. I'm glad they're getting the education they deserve."

"Yeah well, if you scream at them enough, they can be real polite. I'm just hoping that stupid dipshit Grady Samuels doesn't throw a spanner in the works. Joe, here, can't see what's coming around the corner. It worries me some, and with Freddy's arrest a few weeks back, we don't look as unsullied as we did before."

"I told you, if the Lord didn't want me to tread this path," broke in Father Joe, "he wouldn't have set me on it."

"What you and the Lord know about human nature could fill a thimble. One of us has to be sensible around here," replied Ma.

"If Grady's not going to give an inch, and I suspect he's not, then neither can we. And we have to keep our noses clean from now on," added Giselle.

"I think we're keeping that foremost in all our minds, Ms Dresner," said Jeremy.

"Did I hear you say 'we,' Giselle?" asked Father Joe.

"Father, I just divulged a part of my life to your students that I try not to think about on a daily basis. I'd say that gives me a vested interest, wouldn't you?"

He and the others laughed.

"Yes, Ma'am. I suppose it does."

"Ma, by any chance do you play chess?" asked Giselle.

"Lordy, not for years. I'm a deft hand at poker though."

"Do you think you could pick up chess as quickly as I could pick up poker?"

'Quicker," laughed Ma. "I like a little wine when I'm gaming though."

"I just happen to have a lovely bottle of Cabernet Sauvignon on the sill at home."

Father Joe sighed. Somewhere in this conversation, he had become invisible. "I don't believe Bindaree will ever recover from this." He looked over his shoulder. "What do you think, Percy?"

This time, Percy showed enough respect not to spit on the church floor, but the sound that issued from the back of his throat conveyed his feelings clearly.

★   ★   ★

Victor Dumagee was pissed off. He had lost his best worker to the priest's bloody Sunday school. Tommy King thought he was going to get into the army, for Christ's sake. Obviously the priest was filling his head with fairy dust. They weren't going to take an Abo into the army, and the boy had been one of his best runners. His brother getting messed up might have frightened him, but so what, that's the life you lead when you're coloured. Victor was still doing good business, but he was only one man spread thin. He needed help.

He was also still sleeping on Chip Robert's lounge, a slap in the face to the priest and that bloody old woman who thought she ran The Res. The truth was, both the priest and the woman were becoming a pain in the arse. If they continued to meddle in his business, he might be forced to deal with them both. The priest might like to duke it out in a boxing ring, but the thought of shutting them up more permanently appealed to Victor's vicious nature. He'd never actually killed anyone, although he had certainly maimed people, but he couldn't imagine it would faze him unduly. He had shot at targets before; a man wouldn't be much different. If the priest ever got to questioning him, he'd simply say that was the way God made him. How could the preacher argue with that?

★   ★   ★

Grady Samuels was pissed off. With the arrest of Frederick Nagawilli, he thought he might finally have found the excuse he needed to slam the door on the darkies' school, but that half-wit Max Harris had decided not to press charges. Not only that, but apparently he was actively helping the priest. Grady was playing with the Rubik's cube on his desk—a meditative exercise he indulged in during moments of severe stress. He used it at home a lot. Living with that moronic wife of his, he often needed some relaxation. At least the way she kept eating he'd be putting her in pine box soon enough, and the sympathy he'd get would surely sew up the next election for him. By then, he'd have found some way to run Macaffery out of town for good. As he twisted the frustrating coloured cubes, he tried to think up scenarios that would bring Macaffery undone. Of course, one more incident like the one with Nagawilli at the market and his work would be done for him. But while he sat back and waited for the church school to implode, Samuels figured it may just benefit him to do a little checking on Macaffery. It was important to arm yourself with as much knowledge about your enemy as you could get.

It did not deter Grady Samuels one bit that Macaffery was a man of God. On Sundays, when he had to sit on those damn uncomfortable wooden pews and listen to the priest drone on—and certainly when the collection plate was being passed around!—Grady appeared as God-fearing as they come, but privately, he thought the whole thing was bullshit. There was no all-encompassing light that filled the world. Grady was an old-school Darwinian who believed humans evolved out of the sludge of lesser beings and lived and fought by their wits alone. He didn't feel like a fraud in attending church. He simply adopted the face his community expected of him. Father Joe Macaffery was just a delusional man hell-bent on defying him. The only thing different about the priest from the many others he had squashed under his boot heel, was that Samuels was pretty sure the man would not yield. Lord knows Grady Samuels wouldn't be defeated by a coon-loving, bible-thumper. He felt sure there was a showdown of some sort coming, and to his amazement, although sure he would win the fight, he felt nervous. Perhaps his nervousness was a harbinger of what was to come.

★   ★   ★

Father Joe lay awake for a long time the night of Giselle's talk. He lay in his hammock, gazing at the sky and sipping his fourth whisky, unable to get over what Giselle had lived through. That she had been the same age as some of his kids only lent further weight to his response. He wondered if his students could come through something as soul-destroying as the Holocaust without becoming as vicious as their persecutors. Most of them were already too cynical and defensive for their age. There was Freddy, who rejected his heritage, right down to the name given to him. Tommy, who was willing to carry a gun in some potentially dangerous hotspot rather than stay in The Res. And Doyle, whom all the kids looked up to, but who, over the past few weeks, had regressed back into being the boy Father Joe had first met—a boy who wanted nothing more than to challenge authority at every turn. He knew Doyle displayed all the classic signs of depression, but the boy refused to be helped. A white child would probably be ordered to do two hours of cognitive behaviour therapy each week, with a side dish of Zoloft. But black kids, he knew, were not given the same kind of clinical attention. Doyle's behaviour frustrated Father Joe, because he knew the boy was capable of so much more. Also, without Doyle's mental compass pointing them north, the rest of the class was floundering. He owed the Lord an apology, not for loving the boy, but for the pride that swelled up in his chest at every milestone the boy had conquered over the past six months. Father Joe now recognised the feeling as arrogance. He was like a little kid who has built a sandcastle, and jumps up and down shouting, "Look, look what I did. Isn't it fabulous?" Well, Doyle's sandcastle had been well and truly kicked over, and instead of helping him, his priest and teacher was wallowing in self-pity and a good Irish vintage.

Father Joe gazed up at the stars of the Southern Cross and yelled into the nothingness, "Hey, you awake, boss? Don't give up on Doyle, OK? There's a lot of good in that boy. If you want to blame someone for being an arsehole, blame me. It's fine. Just give the lad a fighting chance. And you know, one day it would be nice if you actually contributed to our little conversations too. Nothing cataclysmic. I'm not saying you have to be overly theatrical. It's just that things would run a lot smoother if you'd only tell me what you want me to do. What do you think?"

"Father Macaffery, are you all right, sir?"

Father Joe lurched upwards in the hammock until it threatened to spill him and the whisky out onto the ground. It was his neighbour Phil Small, who had been locking up when he heard the priest yelling into the night sky and thought it only considerate to ask him if everything was OK.

Poor Phil topped out at about five-foot-four and sixty kilos wringing wet. He wasn't a churchgoer, but he had never given Father Joe a moment's trouble as a neighbour. Through piecemeal conversation over the past three years, Father Joe had learned Phil was not one of the world's big thinkers, and indeed, with the light of the porch shining on his face, Phil looked plenty perplexed.

He probably thinks I've flipped my lid, thought Father Joe, *and who's to say I haven't?* "Sorry, Phil. I didn't realise I was being so loud. I was praying, and I guess I got carried away. It's not unusual for people in my profession. We can never be accused of talking to ourselves, though, which I believe is a precursor to madness." He could hear himself babbling, but he seemed powerless to stop it, and damn if Phil didn't look even more uncertain now.

"If you're sure, Father. If you need anything, just come on over and knock."

"Mighty kind of you Phil, but I'll be all right. I'm going to finish my drink and head to bed myself. Night."

"Good night, Father." Phil went back inside, no shrewder for their exchange. His offer of help had been pure politeness. Phil only hoped the Father was smart enough to understand that.

He knew, of course, about the school and the priest's strange rebellion, but he had decided the less he knew, the better off he'd be. What he knew of the Father before tonight pointed to him being a pretty decent bloke, but Phil lived under the radar. Unlike the priest, he had never stood toe-to-toe with anyone in his life, and he couldn't imagine anything that might rouse enough emotion in him to do so. He lived simply, in camouflage, and he couldn't allow the priest's quest to flush him out into the open where the world got loud and unpredictable and he might be forced to pick a side. No, if he wanted drama in his life, he'd watch CSI.

CHAPTER 11

Father Joe hadn't had a hangover in three years, until the morning he realised just why he had been avoiding one. The bottle was damning evidence. It had been three quarters full yesterday morning, but now there was barely an inch left. He found four aspirin in the medicine chest, put on coffee and entered the bathroom, where he dunked his head in a basin of cold water. He was towel drying his hair when he heard the front door slam.

"Is that the man coming to tell me I've won Lotto, in which case, I'm buying a yacht this morning and sailing to Fiji? Or could it possibly be Gunther Pearce?"

"Good morning, Father," Gunther yelled through the door.

"The verdict's still out on that." Father Joe returned to the kitchen, and Gunther groaned at the sight of him.

"Oh, Father. You don't look well."

"Son, I'm not well. I did something last night I haven't done for a very long time. I got rotten drunk."

"Because of what Ms Dresner told us?"

"I think that was part of it. Yes."

"Would the other part be about Doyle?" asked the boy.

"You're very perceptive, Gunther."

"I think I know how you feel. I kept waiting for him to put his hand up and ask her something. I mean, it's Doyle, Father. He had to have about a dozen questions flying around in his head at once, but he just sat there. I don't get it. I'll tell you something, Father: he acts like he doesn't care if he's at school or not, but he does. To Doyle, leaving the school would be the same as someone telling him he's just like his father."

Father Joe poured a second cup of coffee. "I guess I better go out to The Res today and see what Doyle's living arrangements are. Last I heard, he and his mother were staying with Alice King, although I know there's been some tension between Tommy and Doyle lately as well."

"Because Tommy knows what he wants and is going for it. The only thing Doyle has shown interest in lately are his poems, and they won't exactly fill a refrigerator when he's older."

"Doyle's writing?"

"Yeah, for a while now. He got angry about that Keneally bloke writing the history of Jimmy Blacksmith. Reckons only an Abo should write the history of another Abo. He says that's why you can't trust exactly what's in that book, because it was written by whitey. Doyle writes poems. Tommy says some of them are real good."

This flood of new information was too much for a hungover Father Joe to deal with, so he donned his wetsuit and headed down to Saxton Beach. He vaguely remembered being a bit argumentative with the boss last night, so he found a nice curl and for the next hour let his problems roll off his back along with the surf. Gunther sat on his rock, listening to what Father Joe considered excruciating noise through his MP3 player, as he watched the Father ride the swell and suck in as much oxygen as possible, after which Father Joe felt infinitely better. It would be some time before he was tempted by Glenfiddich again. The Father usually exercised an almost neurotic restraint over his drinking—an obsession fashioned from years of living with a chronic alcoholic. He was deeply ashamed he had let that restraint slip, especially because Gunther knew about it. Still, the best thing he could do now was to arm himself with aspirin, visit Ma, and get back to his students. He would not let anybody else suffer because of his stupidity. As he came out of the water, Gunther fell into step beside him.

"You know, I had trouble sleeping last night too, after what she told us," he said.

Father Joe reached out and ruffled the boy's wayward curls affectionately.

"Thanks, Gunther. We better go and see how the rest of the class fared."

When Ma dropped off the kids, she informed him she and Giselle had knocked back two excellent bottles of Cab Sav and sat up into the early hours talking. Not a lot of chess or poker was played, apparently. And while some might think of them as the proverbial odd couple, it turned out that they had developed tremendous respect for one another. Father Joe knew from experience just how difficult it was to get Ma's respect, and he was delighted that his two good friends and sources of counsel had befriended each other. However, Ma also delivered news that made him cringe. Sue Roberts and Doyle had moved back home with the abusive Chip, and Victor Dumagee was still holed up in the Robert's house.

Father Joe combed every surface of his mind, but couldn't seem to come up with a solution to Doyle's problems. Gunther was right: school, even with its romantic complications, must have been a respite for the boy. It was useless trying to talk to Chip, or to the beaten-down Sue. He could only reassure Doyle that he was where he belonged, and that the Father was available should Doyle need to talk. The situation made him feel useless.

When he entered the church, the class was uncommonly quiet, as if they too were suffering a hangover from the rare events of yesterday afternoon. He noticed Doyle was sitting at the front of the class rather than with Tommy, who sat next to his younger brother. Doyle was writing in an exercise book that he quickly folded and stuffed into his back pocket when Father Joe entered. The whole class looked as if they were waiting for someone else to speak first. In what he considered a freak occurrence, even Mudguard was silent, his eyes forward, his wayward hand still on his desk.

"OK, we got a specialised lesson in prejudice yesterday. What did you think of Ms Dresner's talk? And don't all speak at once."

The joke fell flat, but as if he had restrained himself for as long as he could, Mudguard's hand rose tentatively. "Father, did I do the wrong thing asking to see Ms Dresner's tattoo? 'Cause, I didn't mean to."

"No lad. You were just being curious. I'm afraid I overreacted a bit there."

The boy nodded thoughtfully.

Jessica spoke from the back row. "Father, I heard about some of what the Nazis did during the war, but I had no idea they were that bad. It was wonderful of Ms Dresner to come and talk about it. I bet she just wants to forget all about it."

"I don't think you can ever forget the sort of thing Ms Dresner went through. Do you all understand why I asked her to come and speak to you?"

There were some nods and some shrugged shoulders.

"I wanted you to understand that while in this country you may suffer prejudice at the hands of stupid, lazy-minded people, that it is nothing compared to what Giselle Dresner went through. Giselle had fewer rights than Rudolf Höss's dogs. I wanted to give you a little perspective, because some of you are just now thinking about what you want to do with your lives and about the choices you have available to you. And you do have choices." He noticed that sometime in the last few minutes, he had captured Doyle's attention. His next words were aimed primarily at Doyle. "I won't have you failing because you've already decided you're going to. If any of you are acting in a self-defeating way, I will call you on it. You'll find life really sucks unless you make an effort. I can assure you the term 'little Aussie battler' wasn't coined by some drunk in a dole queue. Giselle Dresner had every skerrick of human dignity stripped from her, but she not only survived, she made a good life for herself. That's a true 'battler.'"

Doyle, who hadn't participated in weeks, was gazing down at his desk. "She's a real hero," he said.

The room was silent, as if the whole class had just exhaled.

Father Joe waited a moment for Doyle's words to sink in. "Doyle is absolutely right. These days when we talk about heroes, we talk about football players and celebrities. Australia has a proud tradition of churning out people we refer to as heroes. Ninety per cent of the people in this country will tell you that Sir Donald Bradman, our greatest cricketer ever, was a bona fide hero. They may be right; I don't know. As you all can attest, I'm not very good at cricket. What I do know, is that the Don never had to worry about having enough food to eat or being gassed to death, or being one of the lost souls whose job it was to carry the dead to the ovens." He looked at Doyle again. "I noticed you didn't ask Ms Dresner any questions yesterday, Doyle. Did you have nothing you wanted to ask her?"

If the boy was aware everyone was staring at him, he didn't show it. "I had questions, Father. But my mind kept asking who was I to be questioning her about one of the worst experiences anybody could ever live through? I'm just some arrogant teenager, so I shut up and listened." Doyle looked back down at his desk.

"I'm sure she wouldn't have thought you were arrogant. In fact, you can give yourselves a pat on the back, because she commended me on having such a polite class. Of course, she doesn't know you like I do."

Laughter followed; the sombre mood had lifted and the class was, if not exactly back to its carefree best, at least in a more comfortable mood. They had been given a rare audience and received an A+ for participation, and their knight-errant had spoken up after weeks of silent hostility. Perhaps things were getting back to normal.

"So, juniors and seniors, your assignment this morning is to write about someone who is a hero to you. They can be famous, or not. You may never have met them or they might live down the street. Whoever it is, he or she must have inspired you in some way."

"Father, do we have to read these out in class?" asked Gunther.

Tommy laughed cruelly. "We all know who yours is, Gunther."

"In answer to your question, Gunther, no, this is not an oral exercise. After all, that wouldn't be fair to Mr King, who will be busy cleaning our kitchen."

Tommy looked suitably put in his place.

By lunchtime, Father Joe's headache was an echo of its former self. He still felt that Doyle's participation in class that morning heralded good things, but the thought of having one of his kids living in the same space as Victor Dumagee filled him with a white-hot dread. He did not have an answer to the situation just yet, but he sent up a prayer that one would present itself soon.

He found Doyle outside, talking to Mudguard, and asked if he could have a word with him. Doyle looked suspicious, especially after their last private conversation, but just shrugged as he followed Father Joe around the side of the church.

"Have I done something wrong again?"

"No, Doyle, but I was hoping that you might do something for me. After Ms Dresner's talk, I think a lot of the kids are still, understandably, curious about the Holocaust. I was thinking this might be our next class book." He showed Doyle the book he was carrying—*The Boy in The Striped Pyjamas* by John Boyne.

"I was hoping you might give it a read for me, let me know if it's suitable. You can say no, of course, if you're too busy. It's entirely up to you. I'd just be grateful for a second opinion."

Doyle's scowl lifted for the first time in weeks. "I'll do that, Father. But what happens if I don't think it's right for the class?"

"Then it's simple: we don't read it. I trust your opinion on this, lad."

The boy smiled as he took the book, and Father Joe decided to put both feet into the water. He pointed to the beaten-up exercise book sticking out of Doyle's pocket. "Are any of those ready to be read yet?"

The boy's smile seemed to stutter for a moment on his face. "Not yet, Father. They're pretty much just thoughts right now."

"Well, I hope I get to read some one day." Father Joe pointed back to the novel. "In the meantime, I want your opinion on that, OK?"

"OK, Father."

Having Doyle back in the fold made a big difference to the energy of the classroom. But with no church duties and no one to see, the Father was pleased to have a quiet night at home. He made a call to Giselle to tell her what the fallout of her talk had been and to credit her part in Doyle's seismic personality shift. As usual, Giselle was modest and unassuming. She did have plenty to say on the subject of Ma Bess, however, whom she thought was Wonder Woman with a dockworker's mouth. Giselle also conceded that she'd had a little headache that morning as well. Father Joe laughed as he put down the phone.

He went through the kid's assignments, eating a salad as he marked them. Some of the results were predictable; some were not.

Singer and actor Jessica Mauboy was Jess's hero. The Crusty Demons were Mudguard's. Ironically, Max Harris was Freddy's. Gunther's was, predictably, Father Joe himself. What he wasn't prepared for, despite his dig at Gunther earlier that morning, was that Tommy King claimed him as an inspiration as well. They mostly gave good reasons for why they felt inspired by the people they considered heroes, but it wasn't until he got to Doyle's that he was blindsided. Doyle had written:

Where we used to live there was a kid next door to us named Sam. He had Downs Syndrome. Most of the kids left Sam alone, including me. He was my age, but he was small, except for his head, which seemed larger than it should have been. Despite the fact that he spoke well, we often didn't understand him (or maybe we just didn't take the time to listen.) One day, Sam showed me a ladies purse. He said he had found it at the local shopping centre. The purse had nearly three hundred dollars in it. If it had been me, I probably would have just pocketed the money, but Sam was determined to give it back to the person who lost it. When we got to the address that was on the license, I sent Sam up to the door to ring the bell. A lady answered the door and was really cruel to Sam, only opening the screen door enough to grab the purse and count the money in front of him, as if he might have stolen some of it. Then she slammed the door on him. No 'thank you,' no 'goodbye,' nothing! Sam was so upset that he started to cry and he pissed his pants right there on the old bitch's doorstep. He could not understand what he had done wrong, and I couldn't explain it to him so that he could. Finally, he let me take him home to his mother. I don't know what happened to Sam after that, but I have never forgotten him. Sam is my hero!

Father Joe read the piece several times, then said aloud to himself, "Boss, please. This is the boy I'm asking you to help."

The next morning, when he stuck his head out the church door, just before he yelled, "Troops!" he noticed that Doyle was holding the copy of *The Boy in The Striped Pyjamas* and showing the book to Lilly. Doyle was looking at the book, but Lilly was gazing at Doyle intently. Being Irish and of a highly romantic nature, Father Joe pulled his head back in like a turtle and decided to give them another ten minutes. It had been his experience that romance needed a nudge occasionally.

When at last everyone was seated in the church-cum-classroom, Father Joe asked to talk to Doyle.

"What have you done this time, dude?" laughed Mudguard.

"He hasn't done anything, Mudguard. Now, get behind your desk, not on top of it like some damn orangutan," said the Father.

Doyle's expression was cautious as they went outside. "What's up, Father?"

"I just wanted to know if you'd started the book yet?"

Doyle's face broke into its crooked grin. "I've finished it. It's only a little book."

"So, what is your opinion? Do we make it a class book or not?"

"Definitely, Father. If I'd been a chick, I would've cried."

"Then class book it is. I have to ring Giselle Dresner, because the Department of Education is not footing the bill for this particular book; she is."

"But she's an old lady. Does she have enough money?"

"I imagine Ms Dresner's finances are her own concern, Doyle. She feels it's very important she contributes to our little school. We shouldn't question how she does it. We should just thank her, and you can do that when you call her at recess and tell her it's a green light, OK?"

"You want me to call her?"

"That's right. It was your decision. Don't worry. I'll be right by your elbow, and Doyle . . ."

"Father?"

"For future reference, a chick is a baby chicken! We speak of girls with a little more respect, got it?"

"Yes, Father."

Doyle phoned Giselle at recess, and after tripping over his many 'Thank you, Ma'ams' he finally managed to report why he had called. Giselle, as always, was patient and solicitous, to the point that Doyle got off the phone and swaggered out into the carpark, proclaiming he had just been talking to Ms Dresner about their new book. Father Joe could only look at him and shake his head, trying hard to contain the laughter bubbling up within.

★ ★ ★

The Father had been rebuking himself for letting go those responsibilities that did not directly relate to the church school, until one Friday afternoon when his guilty conscience drove him, and an excited Gunther, to the basketball courts where the Father used to umpire the weekly basketball game. They hadn't been there in weeks, but they were met by the same teens he had coached before his job as a teacher had become all-consuming. Gunther walked up to them and put up his hand for a high-five. His hand was left dangling in mid-air. As a member of the team, this was not the greeting he usually received. A perplexed expression crossed his face as the other boys, all white, huddled behind their captain, Nigel Tomlinson's son, Ben.

Father Joe had a bad feeling about this. "Hello, guys. I apologise for not being here for a while. Are you up for a game this afternoon?"

Eight of the boys looked anywhere but at the priest. However, Ben Tomlinson looked at Gunther first, then back at Father Joe.

"We're having a game, Father Macaffery, but I'm afraid Gunther can't play."

Father Joe swore inwardly.

Ben stood there on the court, the ball under his arm, looking back at him with twice the composure his father had displayed in church.

"May I ask why Gunther can't play? He's a member of this team."

"Not anymore. There are no Abos on our team. In fact, we don't want them on our court." The cocky teenager stared at a tortured-looking Gunther. "Sorry, Gunther, but this is just the way it has to be."

Father Joe had to remind himself he was dealing with children, lest his anger boil over. Even so, some of his fury must have been apparent, because the pimply youth and his posse took an involuntary step back.

In a quiet, measured voice, Father Joe said, "You disappoint me, Ben." Looking at each of them in turn, so they knew none of them was exempt from his judgement, he continued, "You all disappoint me. Very much! There was a time, not so long ago, when you greeted Gunther as a friend. He has done nothing to warrant this kind of treatment. I propose you all think about this very carefully, because if Gunther can't play on this team, then you lose your coach as well."

The other boys looked embarrassed, but Ben Tomlinson was unflappable, and he was their anchor. "I'm sorry if you're disappointed, Father Macaffery. It seems like a lot of folks feel that way at the moment. We don't want to, but we can get along without a coach if we have to."

Gunther grabbed Father Joe's arm and said in a strangled voice, "You stay, Father. I'll be all right."

Father Joe watched as Gunther ran off the court, sprinting down Main Street. Then he turned to the now-exclusively white team. "One day, you're going to look back on your behaviour today and you're going to feel ashamed. And do you know something? You should." He walked back to his car alone.

He had a good idea where Gunther would go, so he drove down to Saxon Beach and parked next to the promenade. Down where the sand met the rocky escarpment, he found a tearful Gunther sitting on the same flat rock he perched on each morning when he came to watch Father Joe surf. The boy, still trying to wipe the tears from his face, watched the priest climb up and said, "You shouldn't have come, Father. You should have stayed with the team."

"Gunther, my friend, I would rather the devil scratch my name in his journal than stay another minute in the company of those arseholes."

Gunther tried to wipe his face on the sleeve of his T-shirt. "But, the team . . ."

"Fuck the team. If they don't want us, that's their loss."

The boy seemed shocked by his reply.

"Did you really think that I would stay there without you, son?"

"I don't know. I guess not. Ben Tomlinson doesn't get up to watch you surf every morning."

"Damn straight! Will you be all right, son?"

"I'm sorry, Father, but I'm angry at them. I know I shouldn't be—it's not Christian—but I can't help it. They made me feel worthless."

"You have every right to be angry. They treated you badly."

"I suppose I should pray for them, but I don't feel like it at the moment."

"Gunther, you're a good person, and what you're feeling is a completely natural response. If you want to pray for them sometime down the line, that's awesome, and more than they deserve. Don't castigate yourself for being human, son. What they did made me angry too."

The boy looked back out at the ocean. For a minute neither of them spoke.

"I'm tired, Father."

"Being angry can be exhausting, even when it's completely justified."

"There are people who feel this way all the time. Those who hate us. How do they live with this feeling every day?"

Father Joe couldn't answer immediately. His young friend did not know that the priest had once been such a person. "I don't know, son. Do you feel like joining me for a spaghetti dinner? You can call your folks from the presbytery."

The boy rewarded him with a wide smile. "I'd like that a lot, Father."

Father Joe decided he would go to the sporting goods store in the morning and buy a basketball hoop.

CHAPTER 12

Grady Samuels was an unusually happy man. The duties of mayor were sometimes restrictive, and often what he wanted to do and what he could do about a thing, were two separate things. For months this had been his experience about the tearaway priest and his church school. But now he was armed with ammunition that would bring the priest, and everything he was associated with, crashing down. In the end, all it had taken was to go over the head of that old wop, Father Gus Passali, Bindaree's last priest, and make a phone call direct to the Monsignor in Brighton—and boy, did his phone call get the old guy in a flap. Of course, he promised the Monsignor things would be taken care of with the utmost sensitivity for the church's position, and as much as he would like to drag Macaffery out for a public flogging, they would be. It was when he was on the line to the Monsignor, and the Monsignor was praying for him over the line (wasn't that rich?), that he remembered his father, a staunch atheist, telling him church types were just like snake oil salesman. Drink with them, laugh with them, but just don't show them your wallet. He wasn't sitting up here in his office, chewing aspirin, because he was scared to show his hand. No, he wasn't bluffing. He was that quiet stranger at the table who has bet small all night and lulls the others into punch-drunk complacency until he gets the hand he's been waiting for and puts everything in the pot. Grady liked that image, even as he battled another skull-thumper of a headache. He signalled the lovely Ms Primrose to let his guest in.

Half an hour later, David Lomado, a reporter with the *Bindaree News*, left Grady's office shaking his head as if he were a pup with a flea in its ear. Lomado was torn. On one hand, the mayor had just handed him the juiciest scandal ever to hit Bindaree. On the other, he and his family attended St Bernadette's every Sunday and genuinely liked the Father; the news 'Greedy' Samuels had just handed him had not altered that opinion. He supposed he would do what journos in this predicament have done ever since man made paper—get very drunk and hand the copy (and thus the problem) to his editor when the mayor told him to. He sent up a prayer for Father Joe regardless. The sleepy little patch of nothing that was Bindaree was ruled by a tin-pot dictatorship, making Grady the most powerful enemy Father Joe could have.

Inside, Grady Samuels was very happy with the way things had gone with Lomado. He had just shot the opening salvo in his spiteful war, and it had been successful. Now that the work was done, it was time to give in to the headache and angina that had plagued him all day. He loosened his collar and his straining belt buckle. Then he pushed his intercom. "Ms Primrose?"

"Yes, sir?"

"I've got one of my headaches, and my blood pressure is sky high. I won't be seeing anyone else today. Once you lock up, you can leave for the afternoon."

"What about Mrs Samuels, sir?"

Good god! If it wasn't that the town saw a married man as a solid citizen, he would divorce the woman and her three chins tomorrow. Last night, she had woofed down three pieces of Lasagne and four gin and tonics. There was nothing like going home from a high-pressure job and seeing grease spread all over your drunken wife's face. He'd have to do something about her in time, especially since he had taken to staring at Ms Primrose's breasts whenever she was in the office, and who could blame him? He also happened to know she was single.

He pushed the intercom once more. "If she has anything to tell me, she can wait until I'm home. Have a nice night, Eleanor."

"Thank you, Mayor Samuels."

He lay down on his chaise lounge and tried unsuccessfully to forget all things Macaffery, the priest who honestly believed he had God on his side.

Well, I'm sorry, Father, thought Samuels. *Your God isn't going to help you out of this one. He's on vacation!*

★   ★   ★

The next morning, as Father Joe waded out of the surf, Gunther fell into step beside him.

"Morning, Father. Killer curls today, hey?"

"Indeed, son. But where was my coffee this morning?"

Gunther spluttered something nervously about his mother wanting him to tidy up his room, and Father Joe laughed at him.

"You've got to get more of a sense of humour. You look tense. What can I do for you?"

"It's about the book, Father. I've already read it. What should I do?"

"What should you do, indeed? Well, what is the first sentence of the book?"

Gunther smiled at him in his goofy manner. "I don't know, Father."

"Son, I watch you up there on that cliff face most mornings, re-reading a book I know you have partly committed to memory. So, you tell me, what do you think you should you do?"

"I think I should shut up and read it again and not tell Doyle."

Father Joe put his free arm around the boy's shoulder and looked up at the sky. "Lord, have I told you I love it when they answer their own questions?" He smiled at Gunther. "C'mon, Macduff. You're still making me that cup of coffee."

★ ★ ★

That Monday, as an anxious David Lomado was exiting the mayor's office, there was once again a tectonic shift in desk arrangements within the church. This one was a lot happier and more raucous (hence more time consuming). Once again, Lilly was seated between Gunther and Doyle, who despite looking tired, had the world's stupidest grin on his face. Tommy wasn't resentful anymore, not since he and Father Joe had discussed plans for him to fly down to ADFA for the two-day orientation. The cost of the two days was being spread evenly between Father Joe and Joseph and Alice King, provided the Father accompany Tommy on the trip. Tommy seemed content to sit next to his brother, Trey, and guide him through a class that often resembled a circus more than a classroom.

Mudguard was the only one not happy with the position of his desk. "Everyone knows that if you're down the front you get called on more than the ones at the back. It's unfair, Father."

"Mudguard, you have your hand up for half the class anyway. You know why you've been moved."

"I have an image to protect, Father!"

"I'm sure you do, and that is why you and your image are going to be seated right there until you get a new pair of glasses. You can't see from the back, and you know it."

"This is discrimination. That's what it is."

But the boy was too good-humoured to offer any real resistance. The truth was that Mudguard had to get good enough grades so that he and Doyle could go up north to the mines and drive the big rigs. Probably because of his diminutive size, Mudguard had a love of all things big. His father had told him that they paid pretty decent money up there, and of course, Mudguard had dreams of going from there to driving Monster Trucks, even if he didn't tell anyone that, especially not Doyle. He knew Doyle and Tommy were tight, but Mudguard had hazy notions of he and Doyle becoming just as close. Like everyone in the class, he looked up to Doyle, and he was glad that they found themselves on a path that seemed intertwined.

★   ★   ★

As happens with all small town scandals, the church school soon slipped down a rung on the rumour ladder when an affair exposed one of the town's officials, and Father Joe learnt that although people might not like a situation, by and large they will live with it before they start burning crosses or donning bed sheets, as long as it means they don't have to do anything more strenuous than voice their opinions.

In the two weeks it took the class to read *The Boy in The Striped Pyjamas*, Grady Samuels had chewed through three more boxes of aspirin but had still not given David Lomado the green light to run the story that would break the priest. He was enjoying the feeling of power it gave him, and he was biding his time.

At the same time, Victor Dumagee put a nine-year-old boy in hospital with a broken arm. He had been using the boy as a runner and found the boy trying to fleece money from him. Still camped at the Robert's home, Victor had conveniently been absent when the police showed up to question him.

In the classroom at St Bernadette's, Father Joe had made his students all re-read the passage in which the teenage sister ineptly tries to explain to the nine-year-old protagonist, Bruno, who the people in the striped pyjamas are. *They're Jews*, she says. When Bruno asks if they are Jews too, his sister explains only that they *are the opposite of Jews*. Father Joe wrote "The Opposite" on the blackboard. Underneath he wrote, "Black/White."

"What you have in this book is racism explained at its most basic level for children. Kids can be taught to fear and to hate, despite it not coming naturally to them; curiosity does, and that is also displayed in the book. Familiarity and friendship are too. So, while we're at this point, I'd like to bring up a personal grudge I have: the use of the word 'whitey' to describe all white people collectively. It is what is referred to these days as 'reverse racism,' but I see nothing reverse about it. It is still saying to someone, you are different, so you are wrong. Any thoughts?"

"We don't call you whitey, Father," said Mudguard.

"And I'm glad. Tommy King, are you going to be a good *black* soldier? Or are you just going to be a *good soldier*, period?"

Tommy's face was the picture of concentration. "I hadn't really thought about it like that, Father," he said. "I reckon I just want to be a good soldier, the same as everyone else."

Father Joe smiled at him. "I'm sure you will be too. What I'm talking about is simply that if you want me to respect you, then you have to respect me first. You can't pigeonhole an entire race of people just because you think they lack a little colour. So, I want you to take the weekend, give it some thought, and we will see where we are on Monday."

They scrambled to get their bags. Father Joe caught Doyle as he was running out the door to the bus. "New runners, Doyle? Have you retired the old ones already?"

"You know what they say about a teenage boy's feet, Father. They never stop growing! Besides, these are pretty cool, don't you think?"

"Pretty cool indeed! Enjoy your weekend."

★   ★   ★

Something was wrong, and they all felt it. It was Wednesday, the third day that Doyle had been a no-show.

"Anyone know where Doyle is this morning?" Father Joe asked. "And I don't want to hear he's doin' stuff.'"

Nobody spoke for a moment, and then Lilly timidly put up her hand. "I didn't see him all weekend, Father. I thought maybe he was sick, but when I phoned him it just went straight through to messages. I must have left ten of them, and he hasn't called me back. Father, could I see you outside, please?" she asked, aware the whole class was looking at her.

"Absolutely."

Outside, Father Joe could see just how conflicted she was. She felt a natural loyalty to Doyle, but she was obviously very worried about him too.

"Father, on Friday morning Doyle gave me this necklace as a gift." She held up a fine gold chain with amethysts set in it.

It was very beautiful, and the priest didn't imagine it had come cheap. "It's very lovely, Lilly."

"It's also far too expensive for someone like Doyle to afford. He said he made some money splitting wood for his father. Father, I love Doyle, but that explanation just doesn't ring true to me. Now he's not at school when he should be. I'm afraid I know what Doyle's doing, and it's dangerous."

"Lilly, I know you love Doyle. I'm kind of fond of the little bugger myself. I will find out what he's doing and if it is what I think it is, I'll put a stop to it. I promise you that."

The girl still looked anxious. "He's going to be so mad I talked about this with you."

"Talked about what with me? I have no idea what you're talking about. Now, go back inside and leave everything to me, OK?"

"OK. Thank you, Father."

Father Joe watched her as she slipped back inside. He had to applaud her courage, because he knew just how shy she was and what a toll it had taken on her to stand up and speak, even when the moment required it. *That's one tree that will bear good fruit,* he thought.

"Tommy, I'm taking a run out to The Res," he said. "Keep them working while I'm gone, will you, lad."

"No problem, Father."

"Do you need some company?" asked Gunther.

"Not this trip. You can come next time, when you've shown me you can master algebra."

Gunther mumbled something under his breath that Father Joe couldn't hear.

"What was that, son?"

"I'm just wondering how often they use algebra in the seminary!"

"Are we going to have a problem?"

Gunther sighed melodramatically. "No, Father. Algebra, it is."

"Good lad. Tommy, don't let this develop into anarchy while I'm gone, OK?"

"I won't, Father."

On the run out to the res, Father Joe wondered what he would find out there. If it were nasty, it was a good thing he was alone. He didn't want Gunther involved. Besides, Gunther couldn't even stay mad at someone who had punched him in the face. Although the Father didn't exactly travel in rarefied circles, Gunther was the only person he had ever met who was totally devoid of malice. He often felt the impulse to wrap the boy in cottonwool, just to shield him from the wickedness of the world, but he also had to admit that he felt a little of Gunther's sheen rub off on him when they were together. On such occasions, he marvelled at what a gift the boy was to him.

It was a very different boy, however, and one that he also loved, who was the subject of his attention today. In his search for Doyle, Father Joe started where he always did at The Res— with Ma Bess.

He was slightly alarmed to find her in her kitchenette, looking very industrious and singing along to Led Zeppelin in full voice.

"Hey, Joe! Tell me, do you know anything about cooking?" she asked. Her buxom frame covered in flour was a comical sight. He also knew that if he laughed, he was a dead man; and they'd never find his body.

"I'm afraid I nuke it in the microwave until it stops moving." He looked around at the flour over everything, the brownish sludge in the bottom of the bowl, and the open bottle of brandy on the counter.

"You're not into the lightning before you collect the kids are you, Ma?"

"I certainly am not, Mr Preacher Man. If it's any of your business—and as usual, it's not—I'm trying to make these." She showed him a recipe for brandy snaps. "Giselle invited me for dinner, and I wanted to bring something nice. When I was there last time, she mentioned she liked brandy snaps, but I don't think I'm doing it right." She pointed to the bowl. "Between you and me, Joe, I don't think this is supposed to be so runny. I don't know, maybe I'm trying too hard to turn myself inside out for this old lady. What do you think?"

"I can't believe what I'm hearing. This isn't my Ma Bess talking. I think trying to make something nice for someone is a wonderful thing to do, and perhaps being a little mindful of some of the language one employs is just good manners. Other than that, you just be yourself. Giselle loved you from the moment she met you. Most folk who meet you love you, Ma. I have it on good authority that the boss does too. As far as Giselle is concerned, your support of the school was one of the main reasons she became interested and got on board. I'm just glad you two are hitting it off."

"Sometimes, I could just hug you, Joe, but I wouldn't want you getting all excited. But if you're not here in the middle of the morning to help me with my cooking, what are you here for?"

Father Joe nodded towards the Robert's place. "Doyle Roberts hasn't been in school since Friday."

"Obviously, you don't think he's at home with a tummy ache."

"No, I don't. He hasn't been reachable by phone, and he's been flashing a lot of cash lately. I've come to hear whatever you know of the situation down there at the moment. Is Victor still there, Ma?"

"Most days, except when he spies a police cruiser. He's got a warrant out for him, but I don't think he's the type to let that interfere with his lifestyle overmuch. I fancy he's paying Chip in either cash or wiz, to stay bunked down there. What are you planning on doing exactly, Joe? 'Cause you got that look a man gets when he's got an itch he's just got to scratch."

"First, I'm going down there to see if Doyle is there, and to see if he's all right. It could be Chip's hit him again, and that's why he's hiding out. I also want a word with Mr Dumagee."

"I suppose I'd just be suckin' used air to say I don't think that's a wise thing to do?"

"Ma, sometimes the wise thing and the thing you've got to do, are two very different things. If you don't mind keeping watch from your window, I'd appreciate it."

"OK, Wyatt Earp, go do your thing. Then come back and let me know what's happening."

The Robert's place was representative of most of the shabby homes in The Res. It had never seen a day's maintenance. The stairs leading up to the porch were on an angle and supported by loose bricks, the front window was cracked, and the pillows on the porch swing were filthy and worn. It was a depressing home, and Father Joe didn't even want to think about what Doyle's private space might be like. No place was really private when you lived with a drunk anyway, he knew. Doyle was smart enough to know that the best way out of The Res was an education, and that's why Father Joe couldn't understand the part of the boy that continued to act in a self-destructive manner. He knocked loudly on the door, trying to be heard over the television that blared from inside. A few moments later, he was faced with a tottering, inebriated Chip, whose demeanour did not improve when he saw who was on his doorstep.

"Fuck me! If it's not the Father! What can I do for you?"

"Mr Roberts, Doyle has missed a couple of days of school, and his classmates and I are a little worried about him. I just came by to see if he was all right. I won't bother you for long, I promise."

For some reason, Chip found this astoundingly funny. "No, you're too bloody right, you won't. This isn't your fuckin' church! This is my home. I say who comes and goes here, and Doyle isn't here right now. I'll be a good boy, Father, and I'll tell him that you want to see him."

"In that case, Mr Roberts, I was wondering if I might have a word or two with your house guest."

"What the fuck are you goin' on about now?"

"Your house guest. Victor Dumagee. I was wondering if I could speak to him?" He was pushing it and he knew it.

Chip's scowl deepened. "I don't have no house guest, Priest. Victor isn't here. He's not here. Doyle's not here. Do I have to draw you a fuckin' picture?"

"No sir, you do not. If you might tell both of them that I need to speak to them, I'd appreciate it. Good day, Mr

Roberts." Father Joe turned and walked carefully down the stairs, not bothering to see what effect his words had on Chip. When he got back to Ma's he could see that she had taken up a position outside, looking down at the Robert's place. She looked expectantly at him. "Well, where's the boy? What happened?"

"Chip Roberts happened. Doyle is with Victor, wherever Victor is now, doing God knows what. I may not be able to find them during the day, but I know where to find them tonight. I'm afraid it's time for Victor and I to have a little heart-to-heart. He's not getting that boy. I won't let him."

"Joe, you know Victor has a gun. Don't go getting yourself shot, is all I'm saying."

"I won't. I promise. What time is your dinner with Giselle?"

"Seven. I must say, despite the brandy snaps, I'm quite looking forward to it. I like her a lot, Joe. She's a very smart woman, and she's surprisingly down to earth. I'm going to get Percy to drive me and pick me up, so I can have a little wine, but I don't want to have to worry about what the dickens you're getting up to, so take care, all right?"

"Why, Ma, that's the closest you've ever come to saying you care," he said cheekily.

"Goddamn it. Before I met you, I never once had any worries over the hide of a white man."

"I'm not white; I'm Irish!"

★ ★ ★

Ma wanted to make sure she looked nice for her dinner at Giselle's, and Father Joe needed some prayer and meditation time to keep a clear head about him tonight, if he was to be successful in bringing Doyle back where he belonged and getting rid of Victor Dumagee once and for all. It was sultry, hot weather, with a storm predicted for early evening, and he watched from the bluff overlooking Saxon Beach as the wind chopped up the surf. He could probably persuade a member of Bindaree's neglectful police force to accompany him tonight if he made enough of a fuss and used Dumagee as a lure, but that might frighten Doyle and make the boy run. Father Joe didn't want that. He believed that if he could only talk to the boy, he could make him see sense. It might be that Doyle would need some counselling of some kind in the future, to help prevent instances like these from happening again, but Father Joe really couldn't think any further ahead than what he was attempting tonight.

The kids knew something was up, too. Ma picked them up two hours early, and they didn't get early marks as a matter of course. Gunther's radar, in particular, was pricked. He had wanted to stay this afternoon, but when Father Joe had told him he needed some prayer time, the boy had backed off instantly. Father Joe had told him he had something important on tonight, and Gunther had looked worried. But as much as the Father loved Gunther, his priority that night had to be Doyle.

★   ★   ★

Grady Samuels had another headache. He'd had this one for three days now and had not been able to do a thing because of it. He was normally a decisive, red-tape-cutting kind of guy, but being hamstrung by pain made him sullen and depressed. The feeling of power he had experienced when he had discovered the information on Father Joe Macaffery and imagined it splashed across the front page of the *Bindaree News* had been a little like taking a drug, but now the drug wasn't working the way it used to. He had hoped not to be incapacitated with pain on the day the story broke, but even on his worst day he was a match for the Macafferys of this world, he believed. When he phoned David Lomado, he caught the journalist just as he was about to walk out the door.

"David, its Mayor Samuels. It's time to run that story I gave you, my friend. On the front page, befitting its scandalous nature. Word it just as I wrote it down for you. And David, I'm grateful you've sat on this over the last couple of weeks. It was very professional of you. You have to realise that the timing of this expose is everything."

David Lomado shook his head and wished he had walked out of the office ten minutes earlier. Regardless of the damage the story would cause, he really hated being used as this fat chump's lap dog. "Mayor Samuels, I'll give it to the editor now. I see no reason why he wouldn't include it in Thursday's edition." Because he felt obliged to, he added, "Sir, I hope you're prepared for a lot of phone calls when this hits the pavement. I suspect the odd person is going to wonder how we let such an oversight happen in Bindaree."

"You do your job, young man, I'll do mine," said Grady, who was not about to listen to a lecture on ethics or responsibility. "After all, that's what it's all about, right?"

Lomado sighed heavily. "Yes, Mayor." He sat down and pulled out the folder that had been buried in his inbox for the past two weeks. The *Bindaree News* wasn't exactly *The Australian* but the job still had responsibilities attached to it. If he refused to print the article, Mayor Samuels would make it his life's ambition to see that Lomado never wrote another word in Bindaree. He needed help. He only hoped that it would be available. He got up and knocked on the editor's door.

"Hey, Al. Do you have a minute? 'Cause I've got myself into something of a situation."

★ ★ ★

Father Joe's plan was to go to the cemetery about ten o'clock. He felt fairly sure he would catch Dumagee there at that time, and Doyle, if he was a runner, would be coming and going from there. But at quarter to seven, he received a phone call that blew all of his plans to hell. At first, he had no idea who had phoned him.

"Father Macaffery, are you there?" asked a deep, sonorous voice.

"This is Father Joe Macaffery. May I ask who this is?"

"It's about Ma Bess. Father, she's been hurt."

"Ma? Who is this?" he demanded.

"It's Percy, Father. I'm in Ma's van with her now. She's been beaten up pretty bad. She insisted I call you. Says she has to speak to you right now. Can you come quickly, Father? I'm calling for an ambulance just as soon as I hang up from you."

Father Joe grabbed his keys up off the desk. "Tell her I'm on my way, Percy. Tell her to hang on."

He roared into The Res twenty minutes later, just as the first fork of lightning split the sky and the rain started to pelt down. Ma Bess was on the floor of her van, with Percy kneeling next to her. He had put a pillow under her head, but Father Joe didn't think anything would lessen the pain she must have been feeling. Victor had come to call on Ma after receiving his message from Chip Roberts, and he had taken his fury and frustration out on her. He had used the butt of his gun to hit her in the face, splitting the skin in several places, and leaving a large gash on her forehead that needed stitches urgently. Victor had hit her in the face, the ribs, and the stomach, and when she had collapsed on the ground, he laid into her with his boot. Her left arm and ribs were broken, and the hospital would have to assess her for any internal injuries.

Father Joe was so mad his vision swam red and he had to swallow the bile that kept rising in his throat. He wanted to do to Victor what he had done to Ma. It didn't help to think that it was probably Chip witnessing Ma looking out for the priest that morning that had made Dumagee target her. Victor was trying to send him a message. In some diseased crevice of the punk's brain, he no doubt thought that this would intimidate the priest. *Victor isn't a very good judge of character,* thought the priest.

"The boy, Joe," Ma muttered through cracked and swollen lips. "He was with Victor. Didn't come up here though. Didn't see this. Be careful, Joe. He's crazy!"

"Shhh, Ma. It's OK. There is no way that cretin is getting away with this." He turned to Percy as the ambulance arrived. "Percy, you go in the ambulance with Ma. I'll follow you to the hospital, OK?"

"Are you still going after that bastard?"

"Absolutely. But I want to see Ma tended to first."

"I'll come with you."

"No. Listen to me, Percy. Your place is by her side tonight. I can't do what I have to do if I'm worried about her. I need you to stay with her, all right?"

For a moment, Percy's face took on the expression he got just before he spat a great globule of phlegm and indignation in the direction of Father Joe's shoes, but it passed, and he nodded slowly. Father Joe could tell he was close to tears.

"I'm sorry. I'm just a silly old man, but I love her very much, you know?"

"I know. So do I."

On the way to the hospital, Father Joe called Giselle and told her what had happened. He didn't want to scare her, so he didn't elaborate on Ma's injuries. For all that, Giselle seemed attuned to the words he didn't say. She asked Father Joe to pick her up and demanded to be allowed to sit with Ma at the hospital. As polite and genteel as Giselle was, she and Ma had one thing in common, they both had wills of iron and it was impossible to say no to either of them.

Father Joe left his three friends at the hospital. Ma was being examined and X-rayed by Doc Wilson and Percy and Giselle were sitting patiently at her bedside, waiting. They both looked worried, but wished him good luck.

It was just after ten p.m. when he arrived at the cemetery, and the rain was heavy enough to wet him through. He was lucky, his last encounter here had pretty much shown him where Victor would be on a night like this, and indeed, he found Victor and Doyle in the same mausoleum.

The two men glared at each other, Victor's face a furious smirk. Doyle focussed on the ground, as if he wanted it to swallow him up.

Father Joe glanced from the thug, to the boy. "Doyle, it's a bit late to be out, don't you think? I don't know what you think you're doing, but the class and I would be grateful if you'd return. We've missed you."

Victor spat at him. "School's out, Father. Doyle's making money now. He's a man now. Isn't that right, Doyle?"

Doyle just stood mute, a picture of misery on a miserable night.

"I hardly think selling drugs makes him a man, Victor. But if you want to teach Doyle what it takes to be a man, why don't you tell him what you did earlier this evening to Ma Bess?"

"What about Ma?" asked the boy.

Father Joe pointed at Victor's chest. "Your friend here went up to Ma Bess's this evening and took his sweet time bashing her senseless. She's in the hospital now. Percy and Giselle are with her. That's the kind of *man* Victor here is going to teach you to become, Doyle."

Victor hissed at him, but Doyle had already turned on the dealer. "Why would you do that? She's an old woman, for Christ's sake. Why would you hurt an old woman?" He used the kind of righteous tone that had won him points in the classroom these past months.

Victor spread his hands. "Look, little bro, she was a nosy woman, OK? She's always in other people's business. I can't have that. Plus, she keeps this bloody fag priest dogging me. She'll be OK. It's not that bad. I promise."

"Want to go visit her in the hospital and tell her and her loved ones, how it's not too bad, Victor?"

"Look, man, why don't you fuck off and leave me and my little bro here to our business?" replied Victor.

"That's not going to happen as long as that boy's at your side."

At that moment, they were all surprised by the appearance of a very waterlogged Gunther, who had approached quietly and now stood there between them, as if he had just been longing for company.

"What the hell are you doing here, Gunther?" Father Joe glared at him.

"I thought you'd be here and I thought maybe I could help," he said sheepishly. He gave an abbreviated smile to Doyle. "Hey, Doyle." He sensed the situation was fraught with conflict, but being Gunther, he just wanted to help his friends.

"Gunny, you shouldn't be here," said Doyle.

"Neither should you. Hey, I've got a great idea, let's all go home," replied Gunther.

But everyone stood as still as statues.

Father Joe looked sadly at Doyle. "Lad, we talked once when you weren't happy at home. Remember I told you that to *be* different, you had to *do* different. You were doing it, Doyle. You were shining, lad. Now you want to throw it all away, for what? To sell this arsehole's drugs? Do that and you'll be living in The Res for the rest of your life. Do you understand?"

Doyle looked from Father Joe to Victor and back again. There was a very real war happening within him, the mortars going off in his heart. Victor grabbed the boy and spun him so they faced each other.

"Are you honestly going to listen to this God crap, little bro'? You and me, Doyle, we're kin. Tell me you don't believe this holier-than-fuck act."

"I find it hard to believe in things I can't see."

Victor smiled slyly at him and wrapped an arm around his neck. "You can see me, little bro, can't you?"

The boy shook off Victor's arm. "No man, I'm sorry. I can't see you. We're not kin, and you know it. We've just been using one another." He put his hand out to Father Joe. "But I can see you, Father, and I'd like to come back, if you'll have me?"

"There was never any question of that, lad." Father Joe smiled at Doyle.

"You fuckin' little shit . . ." cried Victor, his words disappearing into the wind as he pulled out the hand gun that was stuffed in his belt. He was enraged, and Doyle, having had the gall to reject him, was the prime target of his wrath. Nobody rejected Victor Dumagee.

Father Joe was too far away. A headstone loomed up in front of him as he leaped forward, knowing he was never going to get there in time.

But Gunther's reaction was immediate. He flung himself up in front of Doyle like a jack-in-the-box. Victor pulled the trigger and the gunshot boomed through the darkened cemetery, even above the noise of the storm. Afterwards, he stood there limply in an unbelieving daze, staring stupidly at the gun in his hand. Shooting a person was indeed different to shooting a target.

Gunther slid to the ground, very still. Father Joe rushed to one side of him and Doyle to the other and Father Joe tried to apply pressure to the wound. A river of crimson flowed out of the boy's upper chest. Father Joe had been around people who were dying before; he knew what it looked like.

"Father?" said Gunther.

"Yes, son. What is it?"

"Could you bless me, please?"

"Of course, son." Father Joe blessed him, all the while smoothing Gunther's curly locks back from his forehead.

"Father?" said the boy again.

"Don't talk. We'll talk when you're better." But when he looked into Gunther's eyes, he saw the knowledge there.

"I would have made a good priest, wouldn't I?"

"Yes, son. The best."

But Gunther didn't hear him. That bright point of light, the light that was everything Gunther Pearce had ever been, weakened to a spark and was snuffed out in a second. Father Joe watched helplessly and then closed the boy's eyes. Leaving a sobbing Doyle beside his friend, Father Joe stood up.

Victor Dumagee was still standing there, with the weapon still in his hand, staring now at Gunther's lifeless body.

Rage boiled up in Father Joe. Kicking the weapon out of Victor's hand, he then advanced on the dealer and drove his fist into Victor's face. He felt something give underneath his hand. He had once killed a man he hadn't even hated, all for a title belt and a fat cheque. Now, he hated—a hatred so bloody it blotted out even his God. Gunther was dead. Gunther—who had been his friend. This man had killed him. He punched Victor again and again. The thug was no match and lay writhing beneath him.

"What kind of priest are you?" cried Victor.

"The kind you never should have fucked with!"

After a while, God told him to stop. And after a while, he did.

In the dark and the rain, the four of them made a hellish sight. The priest, tears coursing down his face, cradling Gunther's body; Doyle, also crying feet away; and Victor, bleeding and broken. They stayed that way for a long time, until it stopped raining. Father Joe sat there, holding Gunther. He looked at Doyle, sitting there crying, all of a sudden looking much younger than his fifteen years.

"Doyle Roberts, I have to tell you something before anyone else gets here. I want you to hear me, lad." Doyle raised his head. "What happened here was not your fault. I want you to remember Gunther the way he was. I want you to forget about my expectations, the expectations of your parents, or of that scum over there." He pointed to the quiet, still lump that was Victor. "I want you to be the man Gunther expected you to be, because he loved you. Be that man, Doyle, OK?"

"I'll try, Father."

"It's all right, lad. You're going to have a lot of help."

CHAPTER 13

After a time, he phoned the police and they came. Father Joe and Doyle had to go down to the station to give their statements. Victor went to the hospital, under guard. Doyle stuck by Father Joe's side, waiting for his father, such as he was, to pick him up. Father Joe hated having to relinquish the boy to Chip Roberts at a time like this, but had no choice.

His thoughts were interrupted by the sergeant speaking to him.

"So, you're still saying that you were acting in self-defence when you hit Mr Dumagee?"

"He had a gun and had shot a boy," Father Joe said.

"If that was self-defence, Father, I'd hate to get you angry."

"It's not wise."

The sergeant was staring openly at him now. "Excuse me?"

"You heard me."

When they were done, a silent, grim-faced Chip Roberts collected Doyle. Father Joe sighed and went straight to hospital to see Ma. She was propped on pillows, her right arm was in a cast, and stitches decorated her head and lip. Percy was snoring on a cot on the floor, and Giselle had nodded off in her wheelchair with her neck at such an unnatural angle it was going to hurt her when she woke.

Ma was wide awake. "Hey Joe, I heard what happened. I guess everyone has by now. How bad are you hurtin', my friend?"

"Pretty bad, Ma. How are you?"

"Oh, they've got me hopped up on morphine. I'm not doin' as bad as I was. Don't look very pretty anymore, though, do I?"

"I've seen you look a whole lot better, that's for sure."

He plunked an ominous-looking brown paper bag down on her bed tray.

"What have you got there, you evil man?"

He pulled a bottle of Glenfiddich out of the bag. "I thought we might finally have that drink together. What do you think?"

"Give Gunther a little send off?"

"I don't know that I'm ready for that, if I ever will be. I could sure use a shot though."

Giselle didn't open her eyes, just said, "Please include me, Father Macaffery, and my sympathies for everything you've been through in the last few hours. That boy was a gorgeous child, and how he did love you. How are you feeling, Ma?"

"Better than you, you silly old duck. You and Percy should have gone home and slept."

"We just wanted to be where the action was. Didn't we, Percy?"

At the mention of his name, Percy sat up mid-snore. "What?" His eyes lit upon the bottle. "Have you got the lightning, Ma?"

"Not me, fool—the Father. You best be nice to him too, Percy. He's had a hard night."

A look of intense concentration came over Percy's face. "I know. Father Macaffery, I'm awful sorry about that black boy who died."

"Gunther Pearce," said Father Joe. "His name was Gunther Pearce."

"Gunther Pearce," repeated Percy, rolling it out in his deep baritone, before nodding.

Father Joe poured the shots, and the four of them drank. It was awkward for Ma because of the stitches in her lip, but she persevered. For Father Joe, the whisky reminded him how tired he was. When the nurse came in to check on Ma a few minutes later, threatening to kick them all out if they didn't put the cap back on the bottle, he took it as his cue to leave.

"I'll be back, Ma. I just need some sleep. After all that toin' and froin'."

Laughter followed him out the door.

"You know, Preacher, you're all right for a white man," she yelled.

★　★　★

Despite his tiredness, Father Joe didn't go home to sleep right away. He was headed off in the car park by David Lomado.

"Father, I'm sorry for everything you've been through in the last few hours. I understand you're something of a hero, but we have a problem that has to be addressed immediately. I've promised my editor we would meet him outside the mayor's office, so can I drive and fill you in on the way?"

Father Joe was putting up his hands to protest, when David said, "Father, I know you're tired, and this won't take long, but it's very necessary. Just hear me out, OK?"

Father Joe nodded. *This had better be worth it,* he thought.

By the time they had pulled into a car space in front of the mayor's office on Main Street, he was as alert as if he were going in front of a firing squad.

"Are you sure you'll be all right, Father?" David asked.

"I will. Are you sure your editor will back you? It's a juicy story to give up."

"I'm sure."

"Then let's go and have a chat with the mayor shall we?"

★   ★   ★

Alastair Crowley, the editor of the *Bindaree News*, was a grey haired, hard-nosed Scotsman, with an energy that came from doing what he loved. He had been in the newspaper game for thirty years and could see a fool coming at sixty paces. He shook Father Joe's hand in a strong grip outside the mayor's office. "Father Macaffery, I heard about what happened. I can't tell you how sorry I am to have to ask you to do this."

In light of what they now knew, Father Joe thought their attitude towards him was miraculous. "It's perfectly all right, Mr Crowley."

"Alastair, please. Let's go pay Old Greedy a visit, shall we?"

Ms Primrose, a voluptuous young woman with violent red lipstick, greeted them and, after calling through to the mayor, ushered the three men into the mayor's *sanctum sanctorum*. Grady's look of surprise quickly changed to extreme displeasure on seeing these men, obviously united, in his office without his having summoned them. He did not like surprises, and he feared his duodenal ulcer would flare up with the stress.

"Gentleman," said the mayor sarcastically, "I gather this has to do with tomorrow's story. Father, has Mr Lomado filled you in? It's quite a shocker."

"I've told him," said Lomado evenly.

"That's why we're here, Mr Mayor," said the editor. "I'm afraid you've gone about this the wrong way, sir. If you want to fix a story in my newspaper, it is judicious, polite even, to speak to me personally about it."

Father Joe saw the mayor's face redden. When Samuels tried to interrupt, Crowley ploughed over the top of him. "Please don't embarrass yourself. Nobody dictates what goes in my paper. Tomorrow, I hope, we will indeed be running a story about Father Macaffery. It will say that he saved a young boy's life and captured a dangerous drug dealer. That is, if we can talk the Father into agreeing with it, because he seems given to absurd amounts of modesty. Your story"—Crowley took the file Grady Samuels had given Lomado and pitched it into the wastepaper basket beside the mayor's desk—"will be filed where it belongs."

Of course, that prompted a tirade from Grady.

For ten minutes, Father Joe listened to the three men thrash out their arguments for him and against him, watching with interest as the mayor's face went from red to purple and the man scrambled in his top draw for aspirin. He realised, only then, the full extent of the mayor's hatred. Now that Grady Samuels knew the truth about Father Joe Macaffery, Bindaree had ceased to be a safe haven for him. Father Joe knew the two newspaper men would not succeed in harassing Samuels into silence. They didn't have to print the truth about Father Joe. All Samuels had to do was pick up the phone and call someone. That someone would talk to someone else, and so on and on. It would be like a brushfire going uphill.

"What would the mayor like me to do?" Father Joe asked.

The three other men looked stunned, as if they had temporarily forgotten that the cause for their disharmony was sitting in the same room with them.

However, the smirk was soon back on Grady's face. "I want you to leave Bindaree, and I don't ever want to see you again. Anything less than that is unacceptable to me."

"I won't leave my students," he said quietly.

"Oh, but that's where you're wrong, Father. You've deceived the good people of this town long enough. They are already sick of your association with the golliwogs. I'll make sure not a single black ever sets foot in that church again. The citizens of Bindaree think you're a joke, and now I can tell them that they're right. Can't I?"

"I've gotten pretty used to being unpopular. I'll face up to the truth, if that's what it takes, but I won't leave my students."

Grady's smile had real venom in it. It was time for him to play his trump card. "You'll go. Because if you don't, I will have no choice but to ask Constable Egan to charge the young Roberts boy with being an accomplice to murder. After all, wasn't he with the dealer who shot your shady young friend?"

Father Joe flinched at the mayor's words. Crowley and Lomado were silent. They both knew they had won the battle, only to lose the war.

"I imagine a case could be made for trying the boy as an adult too." Grady's purple-red face wore an ominous sneer.

"You'd do that?"

"Absolutely. You've made this whole town a laughing stock. You've had your fun, and now you have to realise it has consequences. We don't need people like you in Bindaree, Father."

Father Joe nodded, as if trying to convince himself of an awful truth. "Gunther Pearce's parents have requested I officiate at their son's funeral. I would like to do that, and I would like to say goodbye to my class. May I?"

"The Monsignor will be here in a week. You have until then."

"And Doyle Roberts?"

"I won't harm a hair on his little black head." Samuels gestured at the two journalists. "You have two witnesses who will hold me to my word. You know, if it were up to me, you would answer for what you've done. Chasing you out of our town doesn't seem enough."

"You feel cheated. I understand," said Father Joe. "But no one wins here, Mayor. Not even you."

"Oh, but I managed to get rid of you in the end, didn't I? That will have to be enough. Now, that's it, I want you all out of this office. Lomado, Crowley, I'm sure we'll be talking again."

They were ushered outside less than a half-hour after they arrived. Alastair said his goodbyes and returned to his office.

"Father, are you sure you won't change your mind about that article," David asked. "You saved that boy's life. I think it would be good if the community knew about it."

"Gunther Pearce did that, not me. He was quite possibly one of the purest souls I've ever come across. So, no, David, I'm not the hero here. I'd rather not get written up as one. Considering what you know now, don't you think it would be false advertising? Can I ask you one question?"

"Anything."

"Do you happen to have a copy of that file your boss fed into Grady's waste bin? I imagine a story like that is pretty tempting to a newshound."

Lomado blushed. "Actually, I did make a copy, but I will be putting it through the shredder the moment I get back to the office. If this gets out, it won't be because of me."

"Thank you, David."

"No thanks necessary, Father. You've done a lot for this town—if only they could realise that.

★   ★   ★

It was Father Joe's intention to go see Ma that night, but when he awoke it was four o'clock the following morning. He lay there for a minute, listening to the awful silence, wishing for one more morning when he might be woken prematurely by a young man's clumsy efforts in his kitchen. He wondered if, with Gunther's death, his heart had finally taken all the pain it could without atrophying into useless muscle.

With no school today, Father Joe went straight to the hospital to visit Ma. Her raucous laughter could be heard down the hallway. He found her talking to a young woman he guessed to be in her late twenties, with short blonde hair in a pixie cut.

Ma smiled when she saw him.

"Hey Joe, come over here. Meet Ruby, she's a community nurse who's going to start visiting The Res once a week, since the majority of our bull-headed folk won't commit to seeing a doc unless some part of their body is actually falling off. Isn't that great?"

"Fantastic, Ma. But are you supposed to be organising things like that in your condition? Can't it wait until you're out of hospital?"

"I'm not dead yet, Preacher. Just a little banged up, is all. Besides I'm blowin' this joint this afternoon. You can't even get a cold beer to help ease your aches in this place."

"This afternoon? Isn't that a bit soon? What does your doctor say?"

She ignored him and turned to Ruby. "You better go now, Ruby dear, before I get into it with the Preacher here. He can be a real stubborn son of a bitch. You've got my number, honey."

Ruby politely excused herself and Ma turned to him. "Now, don't go getting yourself all in a lather, Joe. That old sawbones who stitched me up is an idiot, anyone can see that . . ."

"But—"

"And as it happens, I'm not going straight back to The Res. Percy and I are going to stop at Giselle's for a spell; not too long, mind, or that bloody place would fall to bits. Percy's gone back to the van to get some of my things. Truth be told, Joe, I think he has a bit of a soft spot for old Giselle. So, now you know all my bloody business as usual, why do you look like someone just threatened your family jewels?"

Father Joe sat down in the seat vacated by Ruby. "Do you know that you're about my best friend in this town, Ma?"

Ma was staring at him in her solemn, unflinching way.

"Joe, why do I get the feeling you're about to tell me your whiskers aren't going to go grey in Bindaree?"

"Because, they're not, Ma. I'm leaving. It's not my choice. Believe me."

"Is it because of what happened to Gunther?"

"He never would have been in that cemetery if I hadn't been there. I have to live with that, but that's not why I'm leaving. Believe me, I would never choose to abandon you or my kids, unless I was given absolutely no choice."

Ma was scowling now. "And that fuckin' arsehole mayor hasn't given you any choice. Is that it?"

"I won't lie to you, Ma. That's pretty much it."

"And there's nothing we can do, Joe?" she asked.

"Nothing."

"When are you leaving?"

"After Gunther's funeral, after I've talked to Mike Potter about the school, and after I've talked to the kids. I don't expect they're going to be very happy with me. I'm one of the first adults, black or white, they've given their trust to, and now I'm deserting them—at least that's how I imagine they'll feel."

"What can I do, Joe?"

"You're mending, Ma. I need you to continue doing that, so you can be strong for them when they need you. But I would like you to talk to Tommy King's father about Tommy going into the defence force. The boy really wants it, and I think it will be good for him. Alice knows it. It's only his father who is on the fence. Since I won't be here to do it myself, I'll also need an adult to accompany Tommy down to Canberra in August."

"Consider it done. If Jack King won't take him, Percy and I will go with him ourselves."

"There's one other thing that's very important to me. Doyle Roberts must have an adult he can turn to outside of that family. He thinks the world of you and Giselle both, and it would be good if you could both put in some time with him. I thought maybe Giselle could hire him to mow her lawn. I'll leave that to you. He really needs a man to talk to—someone like young

Freddy has in Max Harris. I know Percy's not a young man, but do you think he'd agree to keep an eye on Doyle?"

Ma's eyes glittered. "Percy will do what I tell him to," she said gruffly.

"Doyle's so smart, and he's so close to getting his education and being able to get out of that house. He just needs to be pointed in the right direction occasionally."

Ma reached out and took his hand. "Don't you worry about that boy, Joe. Leave him to me and Percy, and Giselle. We'll make sure he's OK." She sighed heavily. "Joe, I can see that warning you you'd get your heart stomped was as useless an endeavour as smoking weed in an outhouse. You're the type of man who invests his heart, as well as his head. Nothing I said could have stopped you."

Father Joe smiled at her. "I am the way God made me, Ma. I suppose you never rule with your heart?"

"I must have decided to at some point, Preacher. 'Cause my heart's sure hurtin' today."

★　★　★

Doyle was furious when he heard the news. "Leaving! He threw his book across the church and stood up. "Oh, this just fuckin' sucks," he yelled.

"Doyle Roberts, I'm not gone yet. While I'm here in this church, you will not use language like that. Now, sit down."

The boy's hands became fists bunched on his hips. "Why. What do you care?"

Father Joe looked from Doyle to the other silent, wounded faces around him. *Can't you see my heart's breaking too?* he thought.

"I care a great deal, boy, and if you don't pick that book up and sit your butt back down at that desk right now, I'll come and assist you. Believe me, you'll feel very stupid if that has to happen."

Doyle's face crumpled. Father Joe knew the boy's ferocity masked tears and that Doyle would rather suffer any torment than admit to that. Not for the first time that day did he send up a silent prayer for strength.

"As I told you, I don't have any choice. Believe me, I would rather stay here and be your teacher for as long as you need me, but I can't. That's that. Does anyone besides Doyle want to say anything or ask me anything?"

Mudguard put up his hand. "Where are you going, Father?"

"I don't know that yet. The Monsignor, my superior, will tell me."

"What about school," asked Tommy. "Is it over?"

"Listen up, all of you, I have just come from seeing Mike Potter. It seems you have especially impressed him over these past few months, on and off the soccer field. Mike has asked one of his teaching staff, Mr Connelly, to continue teaching you here in this church. Ma Bess, once she is well, will continue to drive you to school. Until then, you will be driven by her friend Percy, as you were today. Max and Emily Harris will continue to bring you your milk and bread. Now, I know what you're probably thinking: Connelly sounds suspiciously like another bloody Irishman. But I've met him, and he's a good bloke. I think he'll fit in here just fine once you show him the ropes."

Doyle raised his head off the desk. "Christ, another bloody whitefella to train." He groaned and the entire class laughed.

"Well, Doyle, Peter Connelly is a few years younger than me, so it might not take you as long this time."

In keeping the school open, Mike Potter was displaying a tenacity that might just surprise Mayor Samuels. It seemed very important to Mike that the kids' education wasn't disrupted, and he had been warm and complimentary when the priest had talked to him.

Freddy stuck up his hand. "Father, does this Connelly know anything about soccer or cricket?"

"You know, Freddy, I can't believe I didn't ask him. But he's Irish, lad, and God never made a finer physical specimen."

The whole class began poking fun at him then. Looking at them, he thought they would be all right. He would have to trust the boss to look after them. The boss and Ma Bess.

★   ★   ★

That night, he had dinner with Giselle, Ma, and Percy. The next day was Gunther's funeral, and he would be leaving Bindaree directly afterwards. They made a solemn bunch, and when Giselle asked if he would like to stay the night he said he wanted to spend his last night in the presbytery, and his last morning in the surf.

He had no idea where he was going, but that didn't concern him nearly as much as how he was going to get through the service the next day. For once, he was appreciative of the church's small attendance record over the past few months. He bade his friends goodnight and went home to his little white church on the bluff for the last time.

The next morning, the sky was spotless blue and a beautiful breeze rode in from the ocean. Gunther's parents arrived half an hour before anybody else. Father Joe said what he could to them. Although they hadn't seemed especially attentive parents, they had loved their only child and now clung to each other in their grief. Folk started arriving quickly after that. All of his kids came—all clean, all wearing shoes and nicely turned out to say goodbye to their mate. Giselle, Ma and Percy; Max and Emily Harris; the smirking Grady Samuels and his doe-eyed wife; Phil Small, and David and Heather Lomado, were all there. A surprising number of parishioners who had stopped attending the church because of the school also attended, including the once highly offended, but now contrite, June Bradshaw. Father Joe was also stunned to see a particularly grave and sober-looking Chip Roberts standing with Sue and Doyle. By eleven o'clock, the church was filled to capacity for the first time in months. He looked at the coffin at the end of the aisle and silently asked God, *Is this really what it takes?*

"On behalf of Edith and James Pearce, I'd like to welcome everyone this morning. I see we have a few more people here than we've been used to lately. All I have to say about that is that it must be Gunther's spirit, working for the good.

"I stayed awake all night last night trying to put into words what knowing Gunther has meant to me. What I realised in the early hours—with the greatest respect to his parents—is that, for a man without much family to speak of, Gunther was family to me. For some reason, which God never informed me of, Gunther liked my company. I was grateful, and tried to deserve his. What perplexed me during our time together was that here I was, a man in his forties who was committed to helping people in the Lord's name, but when it came to being filled with the Holy Spirit, this teenage boy eclipsed me completely. Many of you would know that Gunther had his heart set on becoming a priest. At the age of fifteen, he already possessed every quality a person could hope to bring to this vocation. He would have been a better priest than yours truly, because he radiated love. If there was something he didn't understand, like the racial unrest that has gnawed at the very spirit of Bindaree, he never got angry about it. He had an enormous heart, and an ability to listen— even when the subject was difficult to understand. Gunther's solution to any problem was the spirit of caring he brought to it.

"He had a thousand-megawatt smile that I only ever saw falter when he thought he might have done the wrong thing. Gunther was a little paranoid about doing the wrong thing, which became a source of cheap amusement to me because he never really did. You probably all know by now, that Gunther died saving another boy's life. One of his friends. He didn't hesitate to put himself in harm's way. He was selfless, even in death. I admit that I've been in a constant argument with the Lord since that night, about why he took Gunther so soon when leaving him here would have made the world so much better for the rest of us. But I realise God doesn't work to my timetable. He takes each of us when it is in his plan to do so. But, as much as I believe my God is a loving one, I'm angry he took my friend from me. And I imagine some of you are too. We can hope that, in time, that anger will lessen, and we will be left with a sweet cache of memories of our son and friend, Gunther Pearce. Believe me when I tell you that is what Gunther himself would have wanted for us all.

"You should know I am leaving Bindaree after this service concludes."

He could see shock on the faces of most of the mourners. Grady Samuels, sitting in one of the front pews, persisted with his jeering countenance until he realised that his wife was crying, along with many others. He hissed something in her ear and the poor woman blanched and dried her tears with a trembling hand.

"The Pearces have very generously given me the gift of Gunther's bible. I will forever remember the children I have taught here in this little church, but I will never open that bible without thinking of the child who taught me."

The service ended, and all Father Joe could hope was that he had done Gunther justice.

Returning to the cemetery was one of the hardest things Father Joe had ever done. When the mourners left and he was officially "off the clock," he returned to the presbytery, sat on his bed, and cried as he had not cried since he was a boy.

Eventually, he was caught off guard by a knock at the door. He was not expecting anyone, but when he opened the door, before him stood a battered Ma Bess, her arm in a sling. Doyle was at her side, and behind him, the rest of his kids.

"I certainly hope, for your sake, you weren't thinking of cutting out of here without a proper goodbye," she said.

"No, Ma'am. I'd be too afraid you'd hunt me down."

"Father, we're sure going to miss you," said Mudguard. "I mean, you can be a real odd dude sometimes, but you're a great teacher."

The rest of the kids all seemed to agree.

Father Joe's voice failed him. He told himself it was the oratory in the church that had done it, but he didn't believe himself.

Thankfully, Ma rescued him. "OK, everyone give the father a hug. I know he's a whitefella, but I don't think you'll catch any cooties."

One by one, they came forward and hugged him, although some of the older boys seemed a little embarrassed and settled for a high-five. Trey King hugged him and thanked him again for rescuing him. They all realised this was their last chance to say goodbye. Finally, Ma gave him an extremely careful hug. He kissed her on the cheek in return.

"Now, don't be getting all frisky in front of the young 'uns," she said. Then, more seriously, "You take good care out there, Joe."

He was about to get into his car when Doyle bolted towards him. The boy's arms clamped around him. "What if I stuff up again? What if I can't do it without you?" he said in an anguished voice.

Father Joe held the boy by the shoulders. "I believe in you, lad."

"I'm going to try to be more like Gunther. I promise."

Father Joe shook his head. "That's not what I want. You just be the best Doyle Roberts you can be. The one I saw day after day in that classroom. He's a good enough bloke for anyone, believe me. God will take care of you, Doyle."

"I don't even know if I believe in God, Father."

"That's all right, lad. He believes in you. We both do. And I'd sure like to be walking past a bookstore one day and see Doyle Robert's name on the cover of a book. Keep writing, Doyle."

★   ★   ★

David Lomado had excused himself early from church, telling Heather he had a task to take care of at the office and that it wouldn't take long. Normally, she would have given him hell about going into the office on a weekend, but the funeral had subdued her usual feistiness and she only nodded and told him not to be long.

David had not lied to Father Macaffery when he said that he would destroy the document he now held in his hands. He had truly meant to, at the time. That he had not yet done it, he blamed on journalistic curiosity. It went against every instinct to kill evidence of what would surely have been the newspaper's most sensational story. Alastair and David had discussed it. They weren't naïve. They both realised the news would leak out to the townspeople eventually—that fat little prick of a mayor would no doubt see to that. But having given his word to Macaffery, David felt an obligation to uphold his end of the bargain. He looked at the document with wonder. Grady Samuels had printed the following in small, tight script:

To the citizens of Bindaree,

This morning, after I had failed to reach our previous priest, Father Gus Passali, I phoned the Monsignor in Brighton, whom I presumed was Joe Macaffery's superior. I wanted to find out if what Macaffery was doing in the church fell inside or out of the church's interests. The Monsignor, who has resided in Brighton and held the same position for the last eighteen years, informed me that neither he nor any seminary that fills positions within the church, recognised the name Father Joseph Macaffery. Indeed, there is no priest named Joe Macaffery. The man we know as Father Macaffery is an imposter.

*The Monsignor told me that he knew of a Joe Macaffery
who was a promising boxer, who years ago had gained
notoriety for being particularly aggressive and for once having
killed a man in the ring. Apparently, Mr Macaffery quit
boxing and Brighton shortly after the death, when he became
acquainted with our former priest, Father Gus Passali, who
became a spiritual advisor and mentor to the dangerous and
unbalanced Macaffery. Macaffery had no family and wanted
to atone for his sins. He entered into an arrangement with
the priest where he would take up a temporary caretaker's
position in St Bernadette's.*

*The Monsignor expressed his doubt that Father Passali had
any knowledge of Macaffery's charade as a Catholic Priest.
Unfortunately, Father Passali succumbed to lung cancer
only weeks ago, so cannot defend his position. Though it
seems likely Macaffery had him duped also. The Monsignor
pleaded with me to exercise a degree of prudence with this
information, so as not to embarrass the church, and while
I will attempt to do so, I am more concerned with just
how Macaffery's web of deceit has impacted the town of
Bindaree. The man is a fraud who has exploited the good
citizens of our town. It cannot stand that he remains in such
a position of trust one moment longer. What lasting damage
his deception has done to the good people of Bindaree, who
innocently put their faith in him, is yet to be fully judged.
But, obviously, this so-called school is a prime example
of the harm Macaffery's duplicity has inflicted upon our
town."*

Mayor Grady Samuels.

David fed the document through the shredder and picked up his coat. Funerals have a way of putting a person's priorities in order, and he had planned a very simple afternoon of watching old movies and making love to his wife. In moments of introspection like this, he hoped he had turned out a good man. He thought he recognised goodness when he saw it, and he believed in his gut that the faux-priest, whatever his mysteries, was a good man. David hoped he would find peace somewhere.

★   ★   ★

Joe Macaffery drove slowly down Angel Street, with his eyes on the rear vision mirror, watching the small knot of waving people by the church growing smaller. Finally, he turned onto Bellington Road and lost sight of his friends altogether. Once again, he was leaving people who were dear to him. Ma had asked where he was going, and as honest as she had always been with him, it hurt him to lie to her.

He said the Monsignor would inform him of his next post, but that he was going to visit his brother in Brighton for a while first. In actual fact, he had no brother, and he had nowhere to go and plenty of time to get there. He would continue to pray for his friends and his students, just as he prayed for the people he met before he came to Bindaree. He thought of Gunther and wondered how long he would carry the stone in his heart. Then he decided that perhaps his pain was a fitting measure of his love, and that he shouldn't wish it away so quickly.

He drove on, through the beautiful, crisp spring afternoon, until he came to the place where Bellington Road intersected with the Coulder Highway. He stopped at the intersection. Joe Macaffery looked east and west along the highway, but saw no cars coming. He leaned forwards and peered through the windshield for a minute. Then he leaned back and picked up the bible that lay on the passenger seat next to him. Six months before, he had written Gunther Pearce's name inside it. Carefully, and with his hand still on the book, he looked up at the sky. "All right, Boss, which way do I go now?"

THE END